'Do you want the downfall of Diakos Holdings to be on your conscience?'

'That's not fair,' Rhianne retorted immediately, her eyes sparking blue flashes. 'That's blackmail. I'll tell you the decision I've reached,' she said quietly, trying to ignore the way her body reacted to his nearness. She really would have to make the rules very clear if she wanted any peace of mind. 'I'll agree to marry you—but with certain conditions.'

Zarek's well-shaped brows rose, and Rhianne knew that he was wondering whether he would like what she had to say. She knew that he wouldn't. Zarek would expect nothing less than a normal marriage, with her in bed beside him every night.

It couldn't be done. All her life she'd been waiting for Mr Right. Zarek wasn't that person. She hardly knew him. He'd almost run her over, and then made amends by offering her a job. But if he thought it gave him some prior claim on her body then he was deeply mistaken.

'Our marriage would be in name only,' she said. 'A pu_____nothing less.'

Margaret Mayo was reading Mills & Boon® romances long before she began to write them. In fact she never had any plans to become a writer. After an idea for a short story popped into her head she was thrilled when it turned into a full-scale novel. Now, over twenty-five years later, she is still happily writing and says she has no intention of stopping.

She lives with her husband Ken in a rural part of Staffordshire, England. She has two children: Adrian, who now lives in America, and Tina. Margaret's hobbies are reading, photography, and more recently watercolour painting—which she says has honed her observational skills and is a definite advantage when it comes to writing.

Recent titles by the same author:

THE ITALIAN'S RUTHLESS BABY BARGAIN
THE BILLIONAIRE'S BLACKMAIL BARGAIN
BEDDED AT HIS CONVENIENCE
THE RICH MAN'S RELUCTANT MISTRESS

THE SANTORINI MARRIAGE BARGAIN

BY
MARGARET MAYO

MILLS & BOON®
Pure reading pleasure™

All the characters in this book have no existence outside the imagination of the author, and have no relation whatsoever to anyone bearing the same name or names. They are not even distantly inspired by any individual known or unknown to the author, and all the incidents are pure invention.

First published in Great Britain 2009
Harlequin Mills & Boon Limited,
Eton House, 18-24 Paradise Road, Richmond, Surrey TW9 1SR

©Margaret Mayo 2009

ISBN: 978 0 263 87412 9

Set in Times Roman 10¾ on 12¾ pt
01-0709-49495

Printed and bound in Spain
by Litografia Rosés, S.A., Barcelona

Dear Reader

I hope you will enjoy reading Rhianne and Zarek's story as much as I have enjoyed writing it. It's hard to believe that this is my 75th book—time has flown so quickly. I'm often asked where I get my ideas from, and quite honestly I don't always know. In the early days of my writing career I always had another story ready in my mind before I'd finished the previous one. These days it takes a little longer, but when the ideas do come they appear in my mind as if by magic. This story was born simply because I thought I'd like a Greek setting and a marriage of convenience—and once I had worked out how Rhianne and Zarek met, the rest fell into place.

Warmest wishes

Margaret

CHAPTER ONE

RHIANNE heard the screech of brakes before she saw the car. By then it was too late. Lost in her own world of misery she had not thought to look before she stepped off the pavement. Urged on by the front fender of the car, she spun across the road and for a few moments lay curled in blessed silence. It was as though everything in the whole world had stopped. No traffic noise, no voices, no birds singing. Nothing except a strange calm. She wasn't even hurting.

Then came the voice. A deep, gruff male voice. 'Why the hell didn't you look where you were going?'

Why the hell didn't she look? Rhianne struggled to turn her head and glare at the owner of the voice. He was clearly the man who had knocked her down. Beyond him was his car with the door still open, the engine still running. 'Why didn't I look?' Her tone matched his for hardness. And why shouldn't it when he was behaving as though she was the one at fault. 'Why the hell didn't *you* look? Call yourself a driver. This is a busy main road. You should have had your wits about you.'

'Are you hurt?'

The belated question angered her still further. She closed her eyes, needing to shut out the handsome face that had come a little too close. The man was on his haunches now, peering at her, making her feel like an insect under a microscope.

'Hello. Can you hear me?'

So he thought she'd passed out! Rhianne snapped her eyes open again and scrambled to her feet. She felt wobbly but nothing appeared to be broken. At least she didn't think so. Her legs still held her up and she could move her arms. Her hip felt a little sore and she guessed she'd be bruised tomorrow, but other than that she was okay.

No thanks to Mr Fast Car Driver.

When she looked about her she saw that a crowd had gathered, each face filled with concern and curiosity. But the only face she saw clearly was that of the man who'd given her his hand to help her up—the hand she had ignored. The man who was now looking at her with a frown digging deep into his forehead.

'It was my fault. I apologise.' Eyes that were neither grey nor brown but somewhere in between looked intently at her. Eyes that under other circumstances she might have found attractive. At this moment in time, however, she saw only the eyes of a man who was instrumental in her having made a silly fool of herself. It hadn't been entirely his fault but she wasn't going to admit it.

She could hear the murmur of voices as the crowd dispersed; they were happy that she hadn't been seriously injured and were now prepared to carry on their daily lives as though nothing had happened.

Rhianne wished that nothing had happened, that nothing had changed, that she was still in the job she loved and that she hadn't made that awful discovery about Angus.

'Apology accepted,' she answered, belatedly realising that the man was still looking closely at her.

'It was, of course, an error of judgement on my part. I apologise most profusely. If there is anything I can do to—'

Rhianne registered for the first time that the man wasn't English. He was olive-skinned and dark-haired—hair that could do with cutting, she noticed, hair that looked as though it wanted to curl, and he had a deep, attractive accent that she couldn't quite place. 'Not a thing. I'm not hurt; you can go, I—' Suddenly the world spun around her, and she put a hand to her head.

Immediately a pair of strong arms supported her, held her against a body that was strong and firm. Even in her woozy state she recognised that this man seriously looked after himself. She drew in a deep, shuddering breath and then wished she hadn't when the scent of his cologne filled her nostrils. She knew that whenever she smelled this same scent again it would forever remind her of this moment.

Smells did this to her. Lavender reminded her of a holiday she'd once had in Jersey, tobacco reminded her of her grandfather. When she was tiny he used to pick her up and swing her around with his pipe still in his mouth.

'You are hurt,' he insisted. 'Allow me to take you home; it is the least I can do. Or do you need a doctor, should I take you to—'

'No, it is nothing,' she exclaimed.

'Then home it is.'

'No!' declared Rhianne, more strongly this time. She had no home; she'd just walked out. She couldn't bear to go back there again.

'In that case I will take you home with me,' he declared imperatively. 'I cannot leave you in this condition.'

'What condition?' she queried, drawing back, widening her attractive blue eyes. 'I'm all right—just a few bruises, nothing more.'

'A good strong cup of tea is what you need, isn't that the English way of doing things? It is my fault that I knocked you down; it is up to me to ensure that you suffer no serious after-effects.'

Rhianne was given no chance to protest further. With her arm firmly held in his, the stranger led her to his car. Another smell, leather this time, she realised as he helped her inside: soft, luxurious leather. It was a big car, big like the man. And expensive.

Who was he? she wondered. She appreciated his concern even though it wasn't necessary. His suit was dark grey and elegantly tailored, his fine cotton shirt was white and his tie the colour of French mustard.

'I can manage,' she declared when he reached for her seat belt. But he ignored her, insisting on fastening it himself. In such close proximity the full impact of this dangerously attractive man hit her with as much force as when he had knocked her down.

Again his cologne filled the air around her. Musky and woody, not one that she had smelled before. It suited him; it suggested a strong male with firm opinions and a sense of what was right and wrong. It was strange how this thought popped into her head. He was making a big impact on her, that was for sure, but she sincerely hoped that she wasn't making a huge mistake letting him take her to wherever he lived.

What did she know about him? Nothing. Not even his

name. Clearly he felt at fault for knocking her down or she wouldn't be here now. But who was he? The effort of thinking proved too much, and she closed her eyes and kept them shut until the car stopped and he killed the engine.

She dared to look about her and saw a tall imposing building. But it wasn't a house, it was a hotel. Alarm bells rang in her head. What purpose did he use it for? Did he make a habit of picking up helpless females?

'You live in a hotel?' she questioned, unaware that nervousness sounded in her voice, or that her eyes had widened dramatically, their normal pale blue darkening to almost navy. She could feel her heart pitter-pattering in her chest and she felt strangely dizzy.

The man smiled. 'In the penthouse suite. Come—' he held out his hand '—let me take you up. I can assure you that you will be perfectly safe. My main aim is to make sure that you have suffered no ill effects. I hold myself completely responsible, of course.'

'It wasn't your fault,' declared Rhianne at once. 'I didn't look where I was going.'

One dark brow lifted, reminding her of her emphatic declaration that he was the one to blame. Nevertheless his voice remained perfectly calm. 'But I should have seen you and made allowances. Let us not talk about this now. Let us go inside and get you that cup of tea. Then you can tell me what it is that was troubling you to such an extent that you didn't see me.'

About to retort that there was nothing bothering her, Rhianne changed her mind. He was probably testing her, trying to find out what was wrong. She had no intention of sharing her problems with a stranger.

As they walked into the hotel, his hand on her elbow,

Rhianne couldn't help wondering whether she was doing the right thing. He hadn't a clue what was going on in her mind. She wasn't after tea and sympathy. In fact she ought not to be here at all. In a state of panic she pulled away from him and would have ran had he not grabbed her arm.

'You're in no fit state to be going anywhere on your own,' he insisted, his voice deep and gruff and very firm. 'If it's me you're afraid of I can arrange for a female member of staff to be in attendance. I can, however, assure you that it won't be necessary.'

His dark eyes looked deeply into hers, and all Rhianne saw was sincerity. She felt faintly foolish and drew in a deep, unsteady breath. 'That won't be necessary.' There were no other words she could find that wouldn't make her look more idiotic than she already felt.

Today had to be the worst day of her life, and receiving kindness from a total stranger when she'd been so badly let down made her feel both grateful and weepy at the same time. Which was not something she was accustomed to. She rarely cried; she'd had the sort of family life that needed strength of character, and she'd always prided herself that she could handle anything.

Now this man was seeing her at her lowest ebb. It did her pride no good at all, and she felt distinctly uneasy as the lift swept them up to his penthouse suite. She stood with her back to the mirrored walls, her hands pressed against it. She could see a dozen images of both herself and the handsome man, each one receding into the distance. She looked absolutely petrified, her auburn hair tousled, her eyes wide with aftershock and fear.

'Is this your permanent home?' she enquired in an effort to break the silence. She honestly couldn't see why anyone would choose to live in a hotel, but he had called it home—so? 'Or are you here on business?'

'It's both. Business is what's keeping me here, and this suite suits me very well. It has everything I could possibly need.'

He had an aura of great wealth—it was in the way he dressed, the way he held himself, his total control and confidence. But there was more than that. Even in her distraught state, Rhianne could see that he was a charmer. She guessed that he probably charmed the hide off every woman he met. He was handsome, suave, good-looking, with a twinkle in his brown eyes that, if she hadn't been in the state she was in, might have affected her senses.

At the moment she was immune to any man, good-looking or not. Rich and powerful or not. She wanted no man in her life for a very long time.

So what was she doing here? Why had she let him persuade her to accompany him? What could he do for her? She wasn't seriously injured, there had been no need for him to make such an offer. And she didn't even know his name. She was accompanying a complete stranger to his suite in a hotel. How foolish was that?

As though he had zoomed in on her thoughts, her companion held out his hand. 'I think it's about time we introduced ourselves. I'm Zarek Diakos. And you are—?'

Rhianne smiled weakly. Zarek Diakos! It sounded Greek, and she couldn't help wondering what business had brought him to England. 'I'm Rhianne Pickering,' she said quietly.

The lift stopped, and the doors silently opened. 'Well, Rhianne Pickering. Welcome to my humble abode.'

Nervously she stepped out on to a deep-piled carpet,

and he led the way through to a living room that was the size of the whole apartment she shared with her friend. She wasn't even aware that her mouth had fallen open. There were valuable paintings on the walls, Venetian mirrors, hand-cut crystal chandeliers. Luxury beyond compare.

'You're renting this?' she asked, unaware that her voice was no more than a breathy whisper.

Zarek shrugged. 'You think it's a little ostentatious perhaps? You get what you pay for in my experience. I can afford it, so why not surround myself with beautiful things? I work hard all day; it is a pleasure to come home.'

There it was again, the word *home*. Rhianne could never imagine calling a place like this home. How could he relax here? There was not a thing out of place. It was a showpiece. Supposedly that was what money did for you. You lost track of home comforts, bought into a life-style that suited your image.

She couldn't imagine living anywhere like this, not even for a holiday. How could anyone get comfortable on those overstuffed armchairs? You wouldn't even want to kick off your shoes and leave them lying around for fear of offending the room's intrinsic sense of order.

'Please, sit down,' invited Zarek. 'I'll ring for tea.'

Rhianne perched on the edge of a chair, and, when he had finished issuing his order, Zarek joined her. 'So, tell me how you're really feeling?'

'Bruised,' she answered on a reflective sigh. 'But other than that I'm OK. I don't really need to be here.'

'You were lucky I wasn't driving any faster. You might not have got away with such slight injury. Would you care to tell me what it was that made you walk out into the road like that?'

'I was deep in thought, that's all.'

'Some thoughts,' he said, his brows rising as though he didn't believe her simple explanation. 'Would it have anything to do with the fact that you didn't want me to take you home? Were you running away?'

'Running away?' echoed Rhianne indignantly. He was too astute for words. 'Why would I want to do that?'

'It's the impression you give.'

Rhianne dropped her head into her hands. 'I have a raging headache. Do you have any aspirin?'

Immediately he sprang to his feet.

It had the desired effect. It stopped him asking any more questions. But her reprieve was short-lived. A glass of water and the tablets appeared as if by magic. He handed them to her and stood over her until she had taken them. 'Would you like to lie down?' he enquired.

Lie down? On a bed? In his private suite? A worst-case scenario raced through Rhianne's head. 'No, I'll be all right,' she answered firmly.

'I could send for a physician.'

'I said I'll be all right,' she said even more emphatically, shooting sparks of fire from her brilliant blue eyes. 'But I would like to use your bathroom.'

'Of course, why did I not think of it?' He crossed the room and opened a door.

Inside Rhianne could see a bed, but nothing else. A four-poster bed! Her heart slammed against her ribcage. She was treading on dangerous territory here.

'The bathroom is to the right.'

It was as if he had read her thoughts, but there was nothing at all on his handsome face to suggest that he had anything other than her well-being in mind. In fact he was deadly serious. Serious or not, though, Zarek Diakos was a dangerous man.

He was as sexy as sin, and she wouldn't have been human if she hadn't felt some reaction to him. Thick dark brows hovered over brown eyes that were seriously striking. Long lashes guarded them. His nose was as straight as a die, very imperial-looking, and his lips were full and wide and mobile. At this very moment they were closed, but she knew that he had beautiful even white teeth.

His hair was thick and dark and touched his collar; his square jaw was darkly shadowed as though he already needed another shave. He was all man; even his body was beautiful. He had taken off his jacket and carefully hung it on a coat hanger in the entrance hall, and through the fine cotton of his shirt Rhianne observed a tangle of dark hair.

Angus had no chest hairs. His body was smooth and clear and—angrily Rhianne dashed all thoughts of him out of her mind. He no longer deserved a place in her memories. She ran through to the bathroom.

Zarek guessed that here was a woman who had more on her mind than the few bruises she had suffered. He went cold every time he thought about what the consequences of the accident could have been. Thank goodness he'd reacted quickly. She had walked out in front of him as though she had had a death wish, and he didn't know how he'd managed to stop without seriously injuring her.

He had a feeling that reaction hadn't yet set in. She didn't realise how dangerously close she had come to being killed. She was an attractive woman with rich auburn hair that curled and waved down over her shoulders, and fantastic blue eyes. It was a shame they were shadowed, and he didn't think it was all to do with the near miss. Something was clearly disturbing her, and he wanted to find out what it was.

Perhaps she would relax shortly and begin to talk. It would do her good. Not that he'd ever been in this position before, but he felt deep down in his gut that she seriously needed to get something off her chest. She had emphatically declared that she didn't want to go home, so it was something that had happened there that was troubling her. And who was he? Sherlock Holmes? He had no idea what was wrong. He was clutching at straws, trying to work something out that had nothing to do with him.

Except that it had. He had knocked Rhianne over and he felt responsible. He even wondered again whether he ought to take her to hospital, get her checked out. Perhaps he should.

Then the tea arrived, and Rhianne rejoined him. After she'd drunk two cups she looked a little perkier. The colour returned to her cheeks, and she even managed a faint smile. It was a lovely smile. It made her whole face lighten and brighten and she looked even more beautiful.

Zarek had had his fill of beautiful women, but Rhianne was—well, she was Rhianne. A good-looking woman with no interest in him whatsoever—which made a change—and a heap of trouble sitting heavily on her slender shoulders.

They drank even more tea, and finally he suggested that he take her home.

The shadows returned to her eyes. 'I can't go back there.' And they filled with tears.

Immediately, without even thinking what he was doing, or that his actions could be misinterpreted, he knelt down and pulled her against him. Rhianne buried her head in his shoulder and stayed there for several long seconds while he inhaled the freshness of her shampoo and felt her hair's thickness between his fingers as he cradled her head.

Whew! He didn't like this, not one little bit. He didn't like the feelings that were beginning to throb within him. This wasn't supposed to happen. He was being a good Samaritan here; sensations like this weren't allowed.

Gently he put her from him. 'Feeling better?'

She nodded, and he reached out a handkerchief, handing it to her so that she could pat her tear-stained face. 'Care to tell me what's troubling you?'

'It's private.'

'And I'm a stranger you're hardly likely to see again. You know what they say about a trouble shared. You never know, you might feel better. I promise not to tell anyone.'

Rhianne found herself giving an involuntary smile. Actually, she didn't feel like smiling, so why it happened she didn't know. Except that this man seemed to understand her needs. It was true, she wouldn't see him again after today. They were passing strangers—even though he had invited her into his house, and she had shared tea with him and buried her head into his shoulder when she had begun to cry.

But to tell him such personal things!

All of a sudden she wanted to. She was filled to bursting with unhappiness, and sharing it with a stranger wouldn't be as difficult as telling her mother for instance. Or a friend. They would ask questions. They knew Angus. They knew she had been planning to marry him. This man would listen and console.

'I don't know where to begin,' she said at length.

'The beginning's always a good place,' he responded,

but she remained silent for so long that he leaned forward and took her hands into his. 'Is it a man who has done this to you?' He asked the question quietly and patiently, not wanting to stir up too much anguish unless she was prepared to confide.

Rhianne nodded, and suddenly tears began to slide down her cheeks, gathering momentum until they were chasing each other in an incessant flow.

Zarek hated to see women cry; it made him uncomfortable; he never knew exactly how to treat them. Though, in all honesty, the women who had cried in front of him had done it for effect. Rhianne was different. She couldn't stop herself. Some man had hurt her like crazy, and she was beside herself with anguish. No wonder she had walked out in front of his car.

Silently he passed her his handkerchief and watched as she dried her tears. He had a strong urge to gather her in his arms and hold her until her sobs subsided. It was an urge he found hard to resist but somehow he managed it. He could imagine her reaction had he given in. She would hate a complete stranger holding and comforting her. Especially a man. She'd quite possibly slap his face.

She needed her mother. Mothers always knew what to say in these situations. He wondered where she lived, whether he ought to suggest he take her there. Even as he thought this, she drew in a deep, shuddering breath and, without looking at him, staring at the carpet instead, she said shakily, 'I lost my job this morning. The company has been taken over and half the workforce has been given their cards. I was secretary to the general manager but it made no difference. I was asked to clear my desk and go, just like that.'

'I see,' he said quietly. 'It's not a practice I condone,

but unfortunately it does happen. Where does your boy-friend fit into this?'

Rhianne shuddered, and once more he wanted to comfort her, but again he knew that it would be overstepping the mark.

'I went home. I was angry and upset. I'd lost a job I love. And what did I find? My boyfriend—the man I was going to marry—making love to my best friend.' And once more she burst into tears.

CHAPTER TWO

ZAREK couldn't stop himself. Rhianne's disclosure had disturbed him, and he took her into his arms and held her close, so close that he felt her heart beating rapidly against his chest, felt the sobs racking her body.

What sort of a man would do such a thing? Not a true and faithful friend. Not a man who loved Rhianne as much as she evidently loved him.

It was none of his business; he'd only just met her and ought not to feel anything, but because he had been instrumental in the accident he felt somehow involved.

'The man's a swine,' he declared fiercely. 'How could he do this to you? He doesn't deserve your tears. He should be strung up to the highest tree. What did you say to him when you found him in such a predicament?'

'I said nothing,' admitted Rhianne, her mouth twisting into a wry grimace. 'I ran away. I couldn't believe my eyes. I felt sick. I just turned around and ran—and why am I telling you this? It's my problem, not yours. I'm sorry, I should be going.' She twisted out of his arms, feeling stupid now for having confessed. And he must think she was stupid for running away instead of facing up to Angus. The truth was she had been so deeply and utterly shocked, so overwhelmingly angry, that words could never have justified her feelings.

'You're going nowhere,' he declared, folding his arms across his chest, his eyes suddenly fierce. 'You're in serious shock, and I don't blame you. What you need to do is devise a plan of action.'

'Action?' queried Rhianne. 'What I'd like to do is march back there and strangle them both with my bare hands.'

'That is good.'

Rhianne dragged her brows together. 'Good? How can wanting to kill someone be good?'

'I mean anger is good. You need to get it out of your system. You need to release it and let it go. Take your anger out on me if you like. Then, when you are calmer, go back and confront these two people who have turned your life upside down.'

'That's easier said than done.' Rhianne's eyes flared a vivid blue, locking with Zarek's steady brown ones, seeing there an understanding that she would never have expected from a stranger. It was hard to believe that she was here in this grand apartment with a man she had met under exceptional circumstances, talking about her private life. She dropped on to her chair.

'May I be permitted to say that your friend cannot be much of a friend if she steals your future husband from you,' he pointed out, sitting again himself, but on the edge of his seat this time, his elbows resting on his knees, his body leaning towards her. 'Was this the first time, do you think? Or are you perhaps wondering how long it has been going on?'

Rhianne's thoughts hadn't even got this far. All she'd

been able to think about was the fact that she'd caught them making love on the living room floor, such mad passionate love that for a few seconds they had not even been aware of her presence, not until she had cried out in anguish.

Then Angus had jumped to his feet, his face a picture of guilt and regret. 'This isn't what you think,' he had said, snatching up his shirt and holding it in front of him.

Rhianne hadn't deigned to answer. How could it be anything different when she had seen it with her own eyes? She hadn't even looked at her flatmate, aware only that Annie had held a shocked hand over her mouth. She had spun on her heel instead and raced from the building, feeling sick with anger and disgust, knowing that the vivid picture of their naked bodies locked together would haunt her for a long time to come.

'I don't know and I don't really care,' declared Rhianne vehemently. 'All I know is that I don't want to see either of them again.' She was still finding it hard to believe that they had both let her down. Her best friend and the man she was going to marry. She put her hand to her mouth and raced for the bathroom again.

Rhianne waited until she had composed herself before rejoining Zarek. In her absence he had ordered a carafe of iced water and, as he filled two glasses, the sound of ice cubes clinking together sounded loud in the room. Rhianne concentrated on the sound, allowing it to take over, to shut out all other thoughts.

Taking her elbow, Zarek led her outside to an enormous terrace with magnificent views over the Thames and the far reaches of London. It was filled with potted palms and flowering shrubs, populated at this moment by brightly coloured butterflies. A haven of peace in the middle of an insane world, thought Rhianne as Zarek urged her in to a padded chair before sitting down himself.

'Are you feeling better?' He was worried about her; she looked desperately pale, still beautiful but with no colour in her skin. It gave her a kind of ethereal beauty, and this woman who had erupted so suddenly into his life intrigued him.

She was such a strikingly good-looking woman that it was difficult to believe that her boyfriend would turn to someone else. If she were his, he would never want to let her out of his sight. Already he felt a strong urge to hold her and kiss her, reassure her that everything would be all right, at the same time taking pleasure in the feel of those full breasts pressing against his chest, her hips against his hips, thighs against thighs.

The thought caused a tightening of his muscles. The worst part was that he wanted to take her to bed, to make her forget everything that had happened. And yet it was this very thing, this act of greedy self-indulgence, that had sent her running.

Disgusted by his thoughts, Zarek busied himself refilling Rhianne's glass. She hadn't answered his question, so he asked her again, 'How are you feeling?'

'Like hell, if you must know,' she declared fiercely, her hands clenching and unclenching on the arms of her chair. 'We've known each other for two years; we're in the middle of arranging our marriage. And now he does this. I hate him. And I hate my friend for being a part of it. I never want to see either of them again.'

'But don't you live with her?' he asked carefully.

'Not any more.' Her eyes flashed angrily and beautifully. 'I'm going to fetch my stuff and move out.'

'Where will you go?' Zarek suddenly realised that he didn't want to let her out of his life. He wanted to help her. It was ridiculous when he didn't know the first thing about her, but fate had brought them together, and he wanted to find out more: what made her tick, what she did for a living, about her family, her mother, her father, brothers and sisters—everything, in fact. 'There's room here.'

He tacked those last words on and then wished he hadn't when Rhianne's eyes opened wide with horror. 'Move in with you—a complete stranger? The man who nearly killed me. Are you insane?'

'It was just a thought,' he said as patiently and non-chalantly as he could. It was a fight to remain calm and impartial when he wanted to offer her the sun and the stars and the moon. 'Of course, you must do whatever you feel is right.'

'I have another friend who'll put me up,' she told him firmly, taking a further sip of water and looking anywhere but at him.

'No family?' It was one of those times when she needed her family around her.

'No!' she declared quickly and tersely, and he didn't follow it up because it was really none of his business.

In one respect he was glad she had turned him down because her big sad eyes overwhelmed him. On the other hand, surprisingly, he wanted her to depend on him. He wanted to tease her back to life, to see those blue eyes sparkling with happiness, to see colour in her cheeks and her mouth wide with laughter. She had incredible lips, full and wide and very, very sexy.

'I'll phone her now.' Rhianne plucked her mobile phone from her bag and walked away from him to the edge of the terrace, leaning on the ornate wall and looking out across the river where life was going on as normal; no one there had had their world turned upside down. She couldn't believe that this man, this stranger, had suggested she share his penthouse. What the hell was he thinking? Strangers didn't make offers like that without an ulterior motive.

He wanted her in his bed, that was what. He thought that because her boyfriend had cheated on her that she would be willing to get her own back by turning to someone else. And although he had to be the most strikingly handsome man she'd ever met, he was too, too gorgeous, in fact—she was definitely not in the market for a quick affair. Zarek Diakos was seriously out of his mind if he had thought she would agree.

Karen answered after only two rings. 'Rhianne, what's wrong?'

Taken aback by her friend's instant realization, she said, 'How did you know?'

'Because you never phone me when at I'm at work. Are you in trouble?'

'Actually, yes,' answered Rhianne, 'but it will wait. I'm sorry, I wasn't thinking straight.'

'Don't you dare end the call,' said Karen at once. 'What's up?'

'I need somewhere to stay for a day or two.'

'Then you've rung the right person. Have you fallen out with Annie?'

'It's worse than that.' Her voice broke.

'Don't say anything now,' urged her friend. 'Tell me tonight. Get your clothes and come round after I've finished work. Are you all right until then?'

'Yes,' agreed Rhianne faintly.

'I have to go,' whispered Karen. 'My boss is giving me the evil eye.'

'Is it sorted?' asked Zarek when she rejoined him.

He looked concerned, a faint frown creasing his brow, his eyes watchful on her face. She wished he wouldn't look at her like that—as though he cared! It was guilt, of course, but even so she would have preferred he kept everything on an impersonal level.

Rhianne nodded faintly. 'She'll be home soon. I'll return to my flat meantime and pack my bags.'

'I'll drive you,' he said immediately.

'That won't be necessary.'

'I think it is,' he stated firmly. 'You need someone with you in case your—er, friends are still there.'

Hot sparks flashed from Rhianne's beautiful eyes. 'I can handle them; I'm over it now.'

'Are you?' he asked darkly, his eyes burning into hers, seeming to see right into her soul.

He knew, she realised, that she hated the thought of returning, but it had to be done. Perhaps having him with her might help. At least she wouldn't have to trundle her cases through the streets; he could take her right to Karen's door. And if Angus should happen to be there then Zarek would be her back up. Even if it gave Angus the impression that she had run into the arms of another man, she didn't care. It would serve him right. He certainly hadn't thought of her feelings when he had made a play for her friend.

She still found it hard to believe that Annie would go behind her back like this. They'd gone through school together, university together. Her betrayal cut as deep as any surgeon's knife.

Unaware that tears were streaming down her face again, Rhianne was shocked when Zarek stood up and pulled her into his arms. Actually, she needed comfort. She needed someone to tell her that it wasn't the end of the world and that one day she would laugh at it.

'Life has a habit of testing us,' said Zarek in his deep, soft voice. 'There are those of us who go under and there are those who rise above it and turn tragedy into triumph. Which category do you belong to?'

His rich dark eyes bored into hers, never blinking, never moving, and Rhianne knew what he expected her answer to be. 'The latter,' she said firmly, resolutely squaring her shoulders.

'Then I have a suggestion which might help you in your hour of need, and it will certainly help me.' He stepped back a pace but kept his hands on her shoulders.

Rhianne looked at him suspiciously. Why did she think that she might not like what he had to say? If he was going to suggest moving in with him again then—

'My secretary is away on maternity leave,' he told her, cutting into her thoughts. 'I've had a series of temps, each one of them as hopeless as the last. The job's yours if you want it.'

Snatching away from him, she stared in total amazement, her blue eyes wide and disbelieving. Why would he offer her a job when he didn't even know her? It didn't make sense. She felt that he would be a devil to work for, and this was why none of the others had come up to his expectations—but to offer *her* the job! 'Is it to alleviate your guilt?' she asked, unable to hide the suspicion in her voice.

When he answered, his tone was clipped and tight. 'I

wasn't the guilty party—you stepped out in front of me, remember. You're lucky I managed to stop so quickly. But it was foolish to think that you'd want to work for me. I take back the offer. Let's go. The sooner you're out of my hair the better.'

Immediately Rhianne regretted her words. She was doing herself a disservice. Where else would she be made such a good offer? 'You took me by surprise,' she said quietly. 'I hadn't even got round to thinking about finding another job.' All she'd been able to think about was Angus's deception, the hurt she'd felt, still did feel. But she had to live; she needed money—why not take Zarek up on his offer?

His face was all hard angles, his eyes brilliantly cold. He stood in front of her like a Roman general, tall and imposing, back straight, chin high. There was no sign of the man who had held her close to his heart, who had caused tiny sensations to creep into her traumatised body.

'Can you reinstate the offer?' Rhianne's voice sounded tiny and hesitant when she had hoped it would be strong. She feigned a smile. 'I wasn't thinking straight.'

'Evidently, or you'd have snapped my hands off. I pay well, but I expect nothing less than perfection. Are you an efficient secretary?'

Don't you think you ought to have asked me this before making your offer? The question formed in Rhianne's mind but she didn't voice it. 'The best,' she answered firmly, taking her courage in both hands and sticking her nose up in the air.

'Then it's a deal. Come, let us go.'

Zarek realised that he had behaved entirely out of character. He didn't normally make offers without thinking them through—so what was different on this occasion? Rhianne Pickering was different, that was what. As well as feeling sorry for her, he was intrigued. He wanted to see more of her, find out more about her, and what better way than having her work for him?

Although he remained silent on the journey, he was conscious of her presence beside him. She was totally different to any other woman he knew, already getting beneath his skin in a way he'd never expected. He was looking forward to working with her, very much aware that it would give him the perfect opportunity to get to know her better.

The block of flats where Rhianne lived were plain and ordinary, and as they went up in the lift to the third floor, standing silently side by side, facing the graffiti-covered doors, he wondered how she could have lived here. She was a classy lady and ought to be spending her time in an equally classy apartment.

He tried not to imagine her living with him in the penthouse, or in his villa in Santorini, but somehow he couldn't help himself. He could imagine her swimming in his pool, all her cares forgotten, laughing and happy, her amazing blue eyes alight with mischief, her white teeth flashing as she smiled into his face.

Glancing at her, he saw the way her fingers were curled into her palms, the way her lips were clamped tightly together, a frown drawing her perfectly shaped brows down over her eyes.

Without even stopping to think what he was doing, Zarek took her hands into his and turned her to face him. 'Are you sure you're up to this?'

Rhianne stiffencd, her eyes evading his. 'It has to be done.'

'Do you think he'll be gone?'

'I hope so.'

'I'll support you if necessary,' he said softly. Although everything that had happened was no fault of his, he felt a powerful urge to look after this woman who had had her world so swiftly turned upside down, who had experienced the worst day of her life, who was alone and vulnerable and needed a male figure to stand by her.

'There's really no need.' Rhianne's eyes flickered up towards his face, and there was a brief second when she held the contact, when something flowed between them, but he never found out what would have happened because the lift doors opened and she turned swiftly away.

He had briefly seen gratitude, but her back was to him now as she turned her key in the lock, hesitating for just a moment before pushing open the door, then, squaring her shoulders, moving inside. Zarek followed more slowly, glancing around the room with interest.

Rhianne had been dreading this moment, and her heart drummed loudly, echoing through her body in painful little bursts. All she could see in her mind's eye was Angus and Annie. Together!

To her relief the flat was empty—she hadn't checked the bedrooms, of course, but there was no sound save for the drum of her heart, and she glanced over her shoulder at Zarek, smiling faintly.

He gave a nod of understanding but remained near the door. He had closed it quietly behind him, not intruding, giving her space and time to do whatever she had to do. She was glad of his presence. In truth, she had been dreading coming back here for fear of what she might find.

But her sense of relief was short-lived when she saw

Angus's tie draped over the back of a chair. Angus was a rep for a pharmaceutical company and always wore suits and ties. Had he left in a hurry after she'd walked in on their lovemaking? Or was he still here?

Annie's bedroom door was closed, and there was no sound, but Rhianne's curiosity took her across the room. Without even stopping to think, she pushed open the door. The room was unoccupied, but as her eyes roved the space she saw further evidence that Angus had been here, perhaps even stayed. A pair of shoes in the corner, the sleeve of a shirt hanging out of the washing basket, and Rhianne knew instinctively that if she opened the wardrobe she would see one of his suits hanging there.

Actually, now that her initial anger and revulsion was over, Rhianne realised that she ought to have seen something like this coming. Angus had always had a reputation for being a womanizer, but she'd ignored that fact when he'd asked her to go out with him, believing him when he'd said she was special. And when he'd asked her to marry him, she had said yes immediately.

Only later, when their wedding arrangements were being made, had she begun to have doubts. There had been whispers that he was seeing other women; she'd actually tackled him about it, but he had convinced her that there was no truth in it, that he loved her and wanted to marry her, and, stupidly, she had believed him.

But to bed her best friend! Why, she asked herself, had she never seen the signs before? How had they managed to keep their liaison a secret?

She slammed the door shut, and immediately Zarek crossed the room and pulled her hard against him. He didn't speak; he seemed to know instinctively that no words would make her feel better.

Rhianne felt his strength seep into her. It was easy to forget that he was a stranger whom she'd met only a few hours ago. He was her saviour, holding her strongly when she felt like collapsing, stroking her hair, murmuring in his native language, finally, tilting her chin with a gentle finger, compelling her to look into his face.

And suddenly he was kissing her—and she was kissing him back! Hungrily and deeply, taking and savouring, her body flooding with alien passion. How could it be happening? How could she react like this when she was still upset by Angus's cavalier attitude? The truth was Zarek's kiss meant a whole lot more to her than Angus's ever had.

Angus had considered himself a lady's man, God's gift to women—which she had blindly ignored—but Zarek was in a whole different league. She sensed that immediately. He wasn't taking advantage of her weakness, he was comforting her. And how!

Her head began to spin, and when he put her from him she clung to the doorpost for support. Wow! A raging heat consumed her, and she was in such a daze that it was impossible to move.

Whether Zarek knew that it was because of his kiss, or whether he thought it was still a reaction to her fiancé's perfidy, she didn't know. But, whatever, he took command.

'Let me help you pack,' he said. 'Where are your suitcases?'

Rhianne ineffectively tried to clear her head. He must think her an idiot standing there with her mouth open and her eyes wide. She pointed across the room, and he dragged them from the cupboard.

'Right, I'll empty your wardrobe, you do the drawers.'

Never had she imagined that she would let a man, a stranger at that, fold her dresses and skirts and place them carefully into a case. She was mesmerised by the way he did it, by the way he stroked out the creases before putting the next garment on top. Until he looked at her, until his dark eyes smiled and teased. 'Do I have to do everything?'

Mentally shaking herself, Rhianne slid open drawers and threw her undies into the other case, going hot at the thought that if he hadn't urged her into action, it would have been his hands lifting her intimate garments. And then the next time she wore them she would have re-membered that he had touched them, maybe even covertly examined them. It didn't bear thinking about.

How one comforting kiss could have sent her into such a tizz she didn't know. Because that was all it had been. He had meant nothing by it.

'You shouldn't have kissed me,' she said, and then wished she hadn't because it gave too much of herself away.

'You were hurting, I wanted to kiss you better.'

'I'm not a child,' she shot back, knowing she was over-reacting but unable to help herself. She had enjoyed the kiss! *Enjoyed it*, for heaven's sake, and that scared the hell out of her! She felt awful. How could this be happening? But worse still, she had promised to work for him. They would be in close proximity for several hours each day. She couldn't do it. Not with the memory of his kiss hanging between them like a tantalising fruit.

'I'm very much aware of that fact,' Zarek informed her, his voice suddenly terse. 'I am merely here to provide support. What happened was unfortunate. If you can put it behind you then the job is still yours, if you cannot forgive me then I will take you to your friend's house, and you will never see me again.'

He paused for a moment, his eyes connecting with hers, cool brown fighting hot blue, and Rhianne knew that she had a hard decision to make.

CHAPTER THREE

TURNING down Zarek's job offer would be both pointless and senseless, realised Rhianne. She needed a job, she needed something to take her mind off recent events, and work would be her salvation. Feeling vaguely guilty now for saying that he shouldn't have kissed her, she said quietly, 'I'd still like the job.'

'Then it's yours,' answered Zarek, his voice calm now, his eyes steady on hers, one eyebrow rising in a crooked arc. 'Although I must warn you that I'm a hard taskmaster. I shall work you long hours, probably longer than you've ever worked in your life, but the rewards more than make up for it.'

Rhianne's eyes widened. 'Rewards?' She needed to know exactly what those rewards were.

'I pay well for good work and loyalty.'

She breathed a sigh of relief, chastising herself for thinking that he might have meant rewarding her by taking her out to dinner, for instance. Or to the theatre. Or even suggest a weekend away. Her mind had run amok at the kind of rewards Zarek might offer her.

If he hadn't kissed her, she would probably never have thought along those lines, and even though she had explained away the kiss to her own satisfaction there was one tiny part of her that knew she must be on her guard at all times. Not from Zarek, but from the feelings that had amazingly risen inside her when their lips had touched.

It didn't take long to finish packing, to drop her toiletries into a holdall, and her shoes into carrier bags. When she was finished, she looked around the room. She had shared this flat with Annie for three years. It wasn't sadness she felt, though, but anger that her friend had cheated on her.

'I'm ready,' she announced crisply.

Zarek's eyes met hers, and he looked at her steadily, saying nothing, simply picking up her bags and carrying them down to his car. He wished that there was something he could say or do to make Rhianne feel better. Her face was deathly pale, and he was afraid she was going to pass out. But he knew that to even touch her again would be a mistake.

She was proudly beautiful in her unhappiness. Her long eyelashes shading her incredible blue eyes, her chin high and haughty, her mouth—well, he preferred not to think about her mouth because he wanted to kiss it again. He wanted to feel its softness; he wanted to encourage a response. Because he had felt a tiny one, even though she had told him off.

Give her a few days, a week or two at the most, and she might return his kisses. Not that this was his prime aim. He felt inordinately sorry for her; he didn't want to see her walking the streets looking for work.

But that earlier kiss had told him that she wasn't immune, and he liked the fact that she was fighting him. In fact, it had been a long time since he had met anyone who intrigued him as much as she did.

The journey to her friend's house was accomplished in silence. Rhianne did not seem disposed to talk, and Zarek respected that. Karen was already home from work, and as she welcomed Rhianne, she looked curiously at Zarek.

But Rhianne didn't introduce them. She simply turned to him and said, 'If you give me your business card, I'll see you at nine sharp in the morning.'

Zarek bowed his head, plucked a card from his wallet and silently handed it to her. 'Do not be late,' he warned.

'Who the hell was that?' asked Karen the moment he had driven off.

'My new employer.'

'You're changing your job?'

Rhianne nodded. 'I've been forced to. I was told this morning to clear my desk and get out.'

'Are they allowed to do that?' asked Karen curiously. 'How does that guy fit into the equation? How did you meet him?'

'It's a long story,' Rhianne answered. 'I need a drink before I tell you. Preferably something stronger than tea.'

'A G&T it is, then,' said her friend. 'And I'll join you. Why don't you put your stuff into my spare room while I'm mixing it?'

As soon as they'd sat down, Rhianne blurted out the events of the day, from discovering Angus and Annie to being hit by Zarek.

'Oh, Rhianne, I'm sorry.' Karen clapped a hand to her mouth, her eyes as wide as saucers. 'What a terrible day you've had!'

'Don't I know it. Luckily I escaped with a few bruises, and that guy who dropped me off was the one who knocked me down. Whether it's because he felt guilty I don't know, but he's giving me a job.'

Her friend's mouth fell open. 'Talk about landing on your feet.'

'It's only temporary, but it will do while I look around.'

'You don't sound impressed,' said Karen. 'He's truly gorgeous. Just the man to get you back on your feet.'

Tell me about it, thought Rhianne. Angus had been good-looking, but Zarek was doubly so. With added charisma. Which would be difficult to ignore. 'I couldn't care less what he looks like,' she told her friend fiercely. 'I'm seriously off men for the foreseeable future.'

'I don't blame you,' agreed Karen. 'I still find it hard to believe that Angus has cheated on you with Annie. Did he really think he could get away with it? I wonder how long it's been going on?'

'I don't think it's the first time he's done that sort of thing,' acknowledged Rhianne bitterly. 'Someone at work told me ages ago that she'd seen him with another woman. He denied it, of course, and I stupidly believed him. He's away such a lot with his job, how do I know what he gets up to? But to cheat with my best friend…I shall never forgive him. In fact, I shall never trust another man as long as I live.'

'They're not all the same.'

'No?' she queried, her eyes rising disdainfully. 'My father cheated on my mother, it's why they got divorced. I always swore it would never happen to me.'

It was late when they went to bed, and Rhianne slept fitfully, thoughts of both Angus's betrayal and Zarek's kiss whirling round and round in her mind. Contrarily, when it was time to get up, she was in her deepest sleep.

The alarm woke her, and she jumped out of bed, forgetting her injuries until she put her foot to the floor. It was stiff and painful, and in the full-length mirror on the wardrobe door she saw a huge bruise on her thigh, a vivid reminder of all that had happened yesterday.

And today she was starting a new job!

She actually felt fit for nothing. She wanted to stay in bed and wallow in her anguish. Both physical and mental. But jobs like the one Zarek had offered didn't come along very often. The salary he'd mentioned was virtually double what she'd been earning. She'd be a fool to throw it away.

Karen had already left, so Rhianne had the house to herself. She showered and dressed carefully in a charcoal-grey suit, teaming it with a white blouse and medium heels. She brushed her thick hair and fastened it up on top of her head, and, with a final glance in the mirror, she pronounced herself ready.

The address was in the centre of the city, and she caught the tube in. Living in London, or even its suburbs, there was no point in having a car—even if she could have afforded one. Limping the last few yards to Zarek's office, her heartbeat quickened.

This job offer had been so sudden, so unexpected, that she wasn't sure whether she was up to it. He was a hard taskmaster, he'd said. Which also meant that she wouldn't have time to dwell on what had happened. This had to be good. So why wasn't she feeling happy? Why was she feeling that she would regret taking on this job?

Diakos Holdings occupied the top two floors of an impressive building. She was shot upwards in a high-speed lift and was evidently expected because she was shown straight through to Zarek's office.

He stood up from his desk the moment she entered. 'Good, I'm glad you made it.' He wore a navy suit and a pale blue shirt and he looked the epitome of a successful businessman. His silk tie was navy also with pale blue polka dots. Everything about him screamed elegance and good taste.

'Did you have any doubts?' she enquired, looking curiously around her once her perusal of Zarek's attire was over. His office was state-of-the-art efficient, cool colours, sleek furniture. There were no paintings on the walls, nothing to take his mind off the job in hand. There was a view over the Thames, but the venetian blinds were angled so that they blotted it out.

'I wouldn't be human if I didn't,' he answered. 'We did meet under rather exceptional circumstances, and my offer of a job was not done in the normal way. I would have perfectly understood if—'

'Mr Diakos,' interrupted Rhianne. 'I gave my word.'

'Of course you did,' he said. 'I should never have doubted it. You're a woman of integrity, and I like that. How are you feeling this morning?'

'Stiff and painful,' she answered.

'Up to working?'

'Of course.'

'Then we'll begin.'

Her office was next to Zarek's with an interconnecting door. In business mode he was very different to the man she had met yesterday.

She discovered that this was the newest branch of Diakos Holdings, and that Zarek was here to oversee things. Their head office was in Athens, and they had other branches in Europe and the United States. It was a world of high finance, and the sort of figures that were tossed around caused Rhianne's head to spin.

He worked her hard, giving her no opportunity to think about her problems and when Zarek said they were finished for the day, she was amazed to see that it was nearly seven o'clock.

'You've done well,' he told her. 'I didn't expect you to keep up.'

'Do you always work this late?' she asked.

'Sometimes later. Is it a problem for you?'

Rhianne shook her head. 'It helps take my mind off...' She tailed away, but Zarek knew what she was talking about and nodded. 'I'd like to repay your hard work by taking you out to dinner. You must be starving.'

Almost immediately Rhianne recalled her suspicions. Her eyes blazed and, with a defiant lift of her chin, she declined his offer. 'My friend is expecting me. She'll have a meal cooked by now. In any case, Mr Diakos, I don't believe in mixing business with pleasure.'

'Of course,' he answered evenly. 'But bear it in mind for another occasion. Dining with me is part of the deal. It would certainly be business because I rarely switch off. You'd find yourself taking notes.'

Rhianne looked long and hard into his dark eyes and saw nothing other than complete honesty—or was there something more? The intensity she saw there made her heart leap and unwanted heat flood her skin. She felt raw vibes crossing the divide between them. With a shake of her head she turned away, picking up her bag and heading for the door. 'Goodnight, Mr Diakos.'

'Goodnight, Rhianne.'

The next few days followed a similar pattern. He

worked her hard, but Rhianne didn't mind, and then on Friday afternoon Zarek asked whether she would be prepared to work the next day.

'Is this what you mean by being a hard taskmaster?' Rhianne asked. 'Seven o'clock every night and then weekends.'

'So it's a no?' A wry smile curved his lips as though it was what he had expected.

'You push yourself too much,' she pointed out. 'Is it really necessary to work on a Saturday? I thought every-thing was up to date.' Heavens, he'd worked like there was no tomorrow every day, what else was there left to do?

'On this occasion, yes, because I have to go home to Santorini. My father's not well, and I want to be on top of things before I go.'

'Then of course I'll come in,' she answered quickly and quietly. 'I'm sorry to hear about your father. Is it serious?'

'I'm sure it's not, but my mother needs me. Will you be all right in my absence? I know you must still be hurting over your fiancé's indiscretions. Have you spoken to him yet?'

Rhianne shook her head, and the pins came out of her hair, causing it to tumble about her shoulders in a cloud of auburn waves. She had always been so careful to keep it neat and tidy for work that she felt embarrassed, putting her hands to it and trying to fix it back up.

'Don't,' said Zarek at once. 'Your hair is your crowning glory; leave it loose. I like it that way.'

He liked it! What was that supposed to mean? He wasn't supposed to like anything about her except her efficiency. Personal issues were not allowed. Hadn't they straightened that out after The Kiss?

'Don't you think you should speak to him?' he asked quietly. 'His defection was a turning point in your relationship. You need to tell him that; you need to make it perfectly clear that he has no part to play in your future—unless you're hoping that—'

'You think I haven't tried?' she cut in crossly. 'His mobile phone's always turned off. He never answers his house phone either. I've even tried going round, but there's never anyone at home.'

'So the whole thing is still an issue between you?'

'I suppose so.'

'How about your wedding plans?'

'I've cancelled them,' she announced firmly.

'And your friend, the one whose flat you shared,' he persisted. 'What does she have to say about the matter?'

Rhianne's eyes flashed a furious blue. 'She's uncontactable as well—if there is such a word. It's my guess they've run away together, gone into hiding somewhere. And if she can't be decent enough to speak to me and apologise, then I never want to see her again.' Her voice rose until she was speaking far more shrilly and loudly than she realised, verging on the hysterical.

Zarek immediately took her into his arms—and, foolishly, Rhianne didn't stop him. The whole issue had been building all week. Not being able to contact either of them was too frustrating for words. She could have thrown herself into the Thames for all they seemed to care.

'You are right, Rhianne,' he said gently. 'They are not worthy of you. Why don't you come to Santorini with me.'

Rhianne felt her heart stop beating. Everything around her stilled. The world grew silent. And then, just as suddenly, she felt a roar in her ears, and she clutched the back of her chair for support.

'I think you know what my answer will be,' she said coolly. 'I like working for you, Mr Diakos, and I like the job, but as for anything else, it's out of the question. I've learnt a huge lesson, and I am nobody's fool. I'm grateful for the job, but if you want more from me, then I'm afraid I will have to quit.'

She snatched up her bag and would have walked out of the door if he hadn't crossed the room in double-quick time and grabbed her arm.

'I have no ulterior motive.' His voice was icy-cold now, his eyes, more grey than brown at this moment, were like flint. 'How could you think like that? I didn't have to come to your rescue. I could have left you lying right there in the road. Your attitude sometimes makes me wish I had.'

'Then you shouldn't make improper suggestions,' she shot back, trying unsuccessfully to snatch away.

'Improper?' He turned her to face him, gripping both her arms, effectively making her his prisoner. 'You have no idea what you're talking about. And if this is all the thanks I get for helping you out then perhaps it would be as well if you did leave.'

He let her go, but he didn't move away, and Rhianne found that she couldn't move either. For some reason she was transfixed to the spot, her eyes locked into his, her wild heartbeat echoing in her ears.

'The offer to come to Santorini was because I thought you could do with a break. There won't be much work for you here in my absence, and I didn't want you to spend time worrying about your broken love life.'

Rhianne began to feel slightly foolish. 'I appreciate your concern, but I really will be all right.'

'Do you still want to quit?' he asked, his tone quieter now, but his eyes remained hard as they looked into hers.

She shook her head. 'I'd be a fool. Good jobs are hard to come by.'

'So I'll see you when I get back?'

She nodded.

He fetched a card out of his pocket and scribbled something on it. 'This is the number of my private cell phone. If you need me, just ring, even if it's only to talk.'

Rhianne's fine brows lifted, and her eyes widened. He sounded as though he really meant it. 'I don't think I'll be doing that.' Nevertheless she took the card and slipped it into her bag.

It was not until she got home that the full implication of what he had done hit her. He was, in fact, offering her a lifeline. He still thought she was cut up about Angus's defection—which she was but was bravely trying not to show it—and he wanted to act as her—counsellor. She could ring him and talk things through; that was what he was saying. He clearly felt involved after the accident. First he had taken her home, then he'd given her a job, and then offered her a holiday in Santorini.

She was sorry to hear his father was ill—it was not going to be a pleasant visit. And she'd done the right thing in refusing to join him. He'd need to spend time with his family, he wouldn't want or need her hanging around. It was not as if they were friends—they were nothing more than acquaintances, really. They'd met by accident, and now she worked for him. Full stop. That was it. Nothing more, nothing less.

When Rhianne went in to work on Saturday morning, she was half afraid that Zarek might ask her again to accompany him to Santorini, and she didn't know whether to be relieved or disappointed when he never mentioned it.

Instead, he was in full business mode, and she felt none of the electricity that had passed between them. It could have been in her imagination, of course, but somehow she doubted it. Zarek was too masculine, too gorgeous, not to let it intrude into his everyday life.

She imagined that most women would fall at his feet, and she probably intrigued him because she was different. It wasn't that she didn't see what a striking man he was—she saw everything—but she had no intention of getting involved with him or any man. She'd lost her trust in men. And Zarek was so incredibly sexy that it would be easy to fall for him—and she couldn't afford to do that. Not to be tossed to one side again when he had finished with her. Admittedly, some affairs lasted, some marriages were happy and lasted, but they were the exception rather than the rule. She had no intention of becoming another statistic. Once was enough.

They worked hard until almost two, and when he had signed the last of the letters, when he had read the last of the reports, he sat back in his chair, ran his fingers through his thick dark hair, and announced that he was finished.

'I don't know about you, but I'm starving,' he declared. 'And as a reward for today you're going to join me for lunch.'

'But—'

'I refuse to take no for an answer.' Brown eyes met and held hers. 'You're a hard worker, Rhianne, efficient, almost second-guessing me. I cannot let it pass. You're having lunch with me.' He pushed his chair back and stood up. 'Let's go.'

Although dining with Zarek was the last thing she wanted, Rhianne knew she was being given no choice. She *had* worked hard, she *did* deserve a treat. When was the last time she'd been wined and dined in style? Not with Angus, that was for sure. He'd worked long hours and they'd usually had either a cooked meal at home or a meal in the local pub.

A public house certainly wouldn't be Zarek's choice. It would be a high-class restaurant where they would get the best treatment and the finest food. It would be nice to be indulged for a change. In truth, she hadn't been eating properly all week, but today she felt that she could do a meal justice.

'You win,' she said quietly.

But her comfort zone was shattered when she discovered that they were going back to his penthouse. 'What's going on?' she asked when his chauffeured car stopped in front of the hotel.

'Why, lunch, of course.' His eyes were full of innocence. 'They do a very good meal here. Simply choose what you like, and it will be sent up. Can you imagine Saturday lunchtime in London? Everywhere will be crowded. It's by far the best solution.'

There was a twinkle in his eyes as he spoke, and they were more grey than brown. Rhianne was fast beginning to realise that brown seemed to be his business mode, or his serious mode, but when he was being light-hearted they were actually grey. And she couldn't help wondering what colour they would be when he was making love. As soon as the thought entered her mind, she dashed it away. She even felt a warmth in her cheeks. How could she even entertain such a notion? Easy, said her conscience. Zarek Diakos is not a man who can be ignored. He's a very sexy individual, and you'll need to be careful if you don't want to get caught in his trap.

So how easy would it be when she was already being led into his lair?

CHAPTER FOUR

RHIANNE was relieved when Zarek suggested they eat outside, and she thanked her lucky stars that it was a hot sunny day. London was stifling, but up here, high above the streets, a light breeze cooled the air around them. And she needed it!

She hadn't felt comfortable with the thought of dining in Zarek's suite. It was far too intimate, especially as the memory of his kiss kept rearing its head. Should he decide to kiss her again, there would be nothing or no one to save her except her own conscience, her own dignity. And would she want to stop him?

Brief though his kiss had been, it had triggered an unexpected and overwhelming reaction, and she wouldn't have been human if she hadn't wondered what it would feel like to be really kissed by him. To feel those strong arms about her, to feel his passion, and, above all—to feel herself responding. She had been shocked to realise how enjoyable this Greek male's kiss had been. Despite its brevity. In fact, it had made such a lasting impression that she had actually dreamt about Zarek making love to her.

In the stark light of day she had despised herself, but here, on this secluded terrace, sipping pre-lunch drinks while the table was set and they waited for their food, Rhianne couldn't stop the loud thud of her heart. Working with Zarek was totally different to socialising with him. In the office she was able to shut out everything except the work in hand. He kept her so busy that she had no choice.

But here, now, when he was acting as though she were a friend rather than an employee, how could she ignore the racing of her pulses, or the heat of her skin which had nothing to do with the heat of the day?

It was a crazy situation; nevertheless, she ensured that her outer image was cool, that not by the merest blink of an eyelid, the flutter of an eyelash, did she let him know how much he affected her. He was her saviour, and that was all. He had given her a job in her neediest hour. And she was grateful to him. But gratitude did not equate to a need to be kissed again. Thoroughly. And satisfyingly. She was ashamed to admit that that one taste had whetted her appetite, and she wanted more.

'You look nervous.'

Zarek's voice intruded into her thoughts, and she looked at him guiltily. 'Not at all. I was actually thinking how fortunate I am.'

'To be dining here with me?' he asked, his eyes twinkling as he deliberately misunderstood.

Rhianne shook her head, unaware that her own eyes were an intense blue, that her rich auburn hair shone like spun silk in the sunlight, and that Zarek found it difficult to take his eyes off her. 'To have been offered another job so soon. If it hadn't been for you, I would be traipsing the streets still looking for work.'

'A lady of your talent? I think not,' he said lightly. 'You've exceeded my expectations, and all I can say is

that your previous company's loss is my gain. I was fortunate to have found you.'

'But did you have to knock me down in the process?'
Humour was the only way she could deal with the situation. It scared her to think how easily she was being
sucked into Zarek's world. Who would have thought that
one day she'd be dining in the penthouse suite of one of
London's top hotels? Or that her host would be one of the
world's wealthiest men? It was like winning the lottery,
as though all her birthdays had come together.

'I couldn't have chosen anyone nicer to run over,' he
said, and there was a gruff inflection in his voice that
hadn't been there before. 'I'm glad you weren't seriously
hurt, Rhianne. And I'm even happier that you've stepped
into the breach. What would I do without you?'

Expressive dark eyes locked into hers, and Rhianne
wondered whether he expected an answer. If he did, there
was nothing she could say. She felt faintly breathless.
She hadn't expected compliments like this. Or was it
because she was on the rebound and read things that
weren't there?

It had to be. Zarek wasn't interested in the likes of her.
He was simply making her feel good because she'd
worked overtime. He'd needed her and she'd helped out.
This was his way of saying thank you. He appreciated
how hard she worked, how dedicated she was to her job,
and how quickly she had picked up the reins. This lunch
was her reward before he went away to Santorini and gave
her time to catch her breath.

Her mobile rang, and Rhianne felt a surge of anger
when she saw Angus's number. 'I need to answer this. Do
you mind, Zarek?'

'Not at all,' he said at once. 'I'll go and see what's happening to our food.'

Rhianne waited until he was out of earshot before she spoke. Even then, all she managed was a clipped, 'Angus?'

'We need to talk.'

'Do we?' she asked coldly. 'As far as I'm concerned there's nothing to be said. You took me for a fool. You thought I was so besotted that I wouldn't mind if you bedded my best friend.'

'That's not true, Rhianne. I love you, I really do.'

'So why did you make love to Annie?'

'Annie came on to me. I told her I was—'

'Don't lie!' Rhianne found it difficult to keep her voice low. 'This isn't the first time you've cheated on me. I was a fool to ever believe your lies. I'm well rid of you, and I pity any other girl who thinks you'll be true to her.'

Angus's tone became suddenly nasty. 'Do you want to know why I looked elsewhere? Because you're frigid, Rhianne. Do you hear me? Frigid! I reckon I've had a close call, and if you're not careful you'll end up an old maid.'

Rhianne heard the click as the line went dead, but she stood there for several more seconds before she found the strength to move. Maybe she was frigid, maybe that was what was wrong with her. Though her own interpretation was that she valued her virginity and wanted to save it for whomever she married.

Was that too much to ask?

She'd told Angus this in the very beginning, she had thought he understood and respected her wishes. It wasn't as though she had never let him touch her. They'd made love in lots of different ways, and he'd said that he found it exciting that he would be making love to a virgin on his wedding night. So what had gone wrong? Why had he felt the need to sow his oats behind her back?

When Zarek returned, he found her sitting with her head in her hands. She looked up at his approach, and her face was pale. 'Whatever is wrong?' he asked at once. 'Have you had bad news?'

'That was Angus,' she said faintly.

'Does he want you back?'

'No.'

'Was he apologising?'

'No.'

'Then the man's a moron and not worth wasting another word on, not even a breath. Are you hungry? Lunch is coming.' Zarek would have liked to say more but it was none of his business. Perhaps, when she'd had time to come to terms with whatever this man had said, she would talk to him.

'I couldn't eat a thing,' she declared.

She had such beautiful eyes; he couldn't bear to see them hurt like this. 'You must eat,' he insisted. 'You need to keep up your strength.' He felt like throttling the man who had done this to Rhianne. First he'd cheated on her, and now he'd said something so awful that she looked as though she was ready to pass out.

Their lunch was brought to them by a succession of waiters and laid carefully on the table. Chairs were pulled out, and they both sat down. At his bidding the young men drifted silently away.

'So what's it to be?' he asked, injecting cheerfulness into his voice. 'A little consommé, perhaps, to start?'

Rhianne shook her head. 'I'd like some wine, thank you.'

To drown her sorrows? He didn't blame her, but they'd

been working since eight thirty that morning; she needed food before drink. 'A bread roll, perhaps,' he suggested. 'Wine on an empty stomach is not good for you.'

He split a roll into two and buttered it before placing it in front of her. 'Now, eat,' he ordered. He kept his eye on her while she nibbled, but not until he was satisfied that she had lined her stomach did he pour her a glass of wine.

As he expected, she drank it quickly and held her glass out for more.

'Is it that bad?' he asked quietly.

'You don't know the half.'

Zarek closed his eyes briefly. He wanted to give her a good shake, tell her to forget what had happened and get on with her life. But he knew it wasn't that easy. 'It's not good to bottle things up, Rhianne, surely you know that?' he said softly. 'But if you don't wish to discuss it, I'll bow to your request. However, I have no intention of leaving you here in this state while I visit my parents. You're coming with me.'

She looked at him as though he had gone out of his mind. 'To Santorini?'

'That is correct.' And once she was out there she would, hopefully, relax. She would forget all about this guy who had carelessly hurt her and turn to him, come to depend on him.

Already his body ached for her. He wanted to kiss her again and again, he wanted her in his bed, he wanted to lose himself in her body. There was no way he could do that while her ex-fiancé still haunted her thoughts, but in Santorini she would become his. He would take it slowly and carefully, his seduction all the more satisfying because of it.

'I can't.' Plaintive eyes looked into his. 'It wouldn't be proper. I—we—oh, Zarek, please don't ask me.'

'Because you know you can't refuse?' She wanted to come, he was sure of it; it was the propriety thing that bothered her. But to hell with that. She needed to get away, and he wanted to find out more about her.

Rhianne was in a different league to other women he'd dated. His wealth did not impress her, nor did she care what she said to him. To her he was just a man. A man who had nearly run over her. A man who was now her employer. But even that gave him no hold over her. She wasn't afraid of hard work; in fact, she seemed to revel in it, but she didn't see him as a potential lover.

Not yet, at least!

It would be his pleasure to persuade her differently.

'My mind's all over the place, Zarek; I need time to myself. I'd be no company.'

'But you do agree that a change of scenery would do you a world of good?'

'I guess so.'

'Then at least let me do that for you. You don't have to spend all your time with me. You can do whatever you like; there'll be no boundaries, no pressure.'

'Would we be staying with your parents?'

'Not at all. My villa is large enough for you to not feel inhibited. You'll have your own rooms and your freedom. You'll be able to recharge your batteries and push all thoughts of your failed relationship out of your mind.'

What he didn't tell her was that he wouldn't be patient for ever. He wanted Rhianne in his bed. Seeing her like this was doing him no good at all. He wanted to crush her to him, he wanted to make love to her for hours on end so that she'd have nothing else left to think about but him.

He watched as Rhianne fought a battle with her inner self, and when at last she spoke, there was nothing on her face to hint at what decision she'd reached. 'I'll come, Zarek,' she said softly. 'But don't expect too much.'

His heart soared. 'All I want is for you to be happy.'

Rhianne frowned. 'Why are you doing this? Why do you care so much?'

Because I fancy you like hell and I want you in my bed. Of course, he didn't say this, he simply gave a gentle smile. 'Because you deserve a break. Because you've worked hard for me this last week, and I want to reward you. Because—well—you look as though you need a holiday. Do I need to go on?'

'You're too kind.' And at last Rhianne smiled.

Zarek felt his heart soar. Rhianne's smiles were heart-stoppingly lovely. She had the most beautifully shaped mouth he had ever seen: soft lips that simply begged to be kissed, and teeth that were white and even. He looked forward to the day when he kissed her again. A proper kiss. One that would shatter his senses—and, hopefully, Rhianne's too.

Rhianne couldn't believe that she had agreed to go to Santorini with Zarek. She felt sure that the only reason he had made the offer was because he felt sorry for her. She oughtn't to have taken the phone call, she ought not to have let Angus upset her. Except that it wasn't nice being called frigid. Her feelings were hurt. She really wanted to be on her own, not here with Zarek, who was being too nice.

But what was done was done. She had a new life to look forward to and a gorgeous man to share it with. At least for the duration of their visit. She suddenly realised that she had no idea how long he intended staying on Santorini. His father was ill he'd said, so possibly there was no time limit. It could be days, weeks, months even. Would he want her with him for that long? Would she want to stay for that length of time?

'I really think you should eat something.' Zarek's rich deep voice cut into her thoughts.

'Maybe I will have a little soup,' agreed Rhianne. Her heavy mood was beginning to lighten. Although the phone call had hurt her, it had also had the effect of bringing to an end one part of her life. And, conversely, a new one was beginning. A life where she made new friends, went to new places, where she could become a completely different person.

'In fact,' she said, 'I'll have a large bowl. I'm suddenly hungry.'

She enjoyed the rest of the meal; a light chicken salad followed the soup, with fresh strawberries for dessert. It was all very light and healthy, and she drank two more glasses of wine, then sat back replete.

Zarek had watched her eating with an amused smile on his face. But he wasn't mocking her, he was pleased to see her enjoying her food. Nor had he done too badly himself. Between them they had managed to finish everything that had been spread out before them.

'You did well,' he said, 'considering you weren't hungry. Did I tell you that my plane flies out first thing in the morning?'

Rhianne's eyes widened. 'Then I need to go home and sort myself out.'

'How long will it take you to pack?'

She shrugged. 'An hour.'

'Then there's no hurry,' he said. 'Stay a while. Relax. Keep me company.'

'Isn't there something you should be doing?' Rhianne wished that she knew why Zarek kept insisting she spend time with him. It was as though he didn't want to let her out of his sight. Perhaps he thought that if he let her go, she'd change her mind about going with him. And perhaps she ought to. There was something dangerous about going with this man to visit his family.

Zarek shook his head. 'Thanks to you we're up to date at the office. I don't even need to pack; it will all be done for me.'

How the other half live, she thought, though she wasn't bitter. Zarek had no airs or graces. He was a man comfortable in his own skin, who had shown considerable concern for her following the accident. She guessed he would help anyone in distress but wasn't he going a little bit over the top suggesting she holiday with him? It was difficult not to wonder whether he had an ulterior motive. And if he had, was she in danger of making a fool of herself, because he was without a doubt the most seriously sexy man she had ever met.

'Come, let us make ourselves more comfortable.'

He pulled back her chair and led her over to the softly cushioned cane seats they had vacated earlier. 'Can I get you anything else? More coffee, perhaps?'

He rested his hand on her shoulder, and Rhianne felt a *frisson* of awareness ride through her, starting in her throat before weaving its way into every part of her body. And it scared her. There were feelings here that she'd felt with no one else. Perilous feelings.

She ought to back out of this situation right now, this very minute. She was treading on dangerous ground, and before she knew it she could be in well over her head.

'No coffee, thanks,' answered Rhianne, and she watched him as he settled himself in one of the other chairs. Not beside her but facing her, which was even more disconcerting.

His dark brown eyes watched her closely, and Rhianne searched for something to say that would ease the situation. Because if he continued to look at her like this, she would end up a wreck. No man had ever managed to disturb her senses to such an extent.

'What's wrong with your father?' she asked, trying to steer the conversation into an impersonal direction. Impersonal for her, at least. Zarek must be very concerned about his parent, otherwise he wouldn't be making the journey.

'He has a recurring heart problem; he's had it for years. I'm not unduly worried but my mother's panicking, so I need to visit.' He spoke casually but his eyes, those eloquent golden-brown eyes, suggested that he would rather be talking about her.

She felt something alien slither down her spine; it was unnerving the way he kept looking at her, and she was surprised when her voice sounded normal. 'I hope she won't mind you dragging me along.'

'Dragging?' Dark brows rose. 'Is that what I'm doing?'

Rhianne gave a light shrug and a grimace. 'I find it hard to believe that I've agreed to go to Santorini with you. It's crazy. We hardly know each other.'

'Then we're going to have fun finding out, aren't we?'

Fun? It was one way of describing it, though it wasn't

exactly the word she would have used. 'But why? Why are you insisting I join you?' she asked. 'It's a family visit not something you should take your secretary to.'

'You're not going to be my secretary while we're away. Oh, no, Rhianne!'

His voice lowered until it became deep and sexy, and what she saw when she looked into his eyes troubled her deeply. 'If you have something else in mind, Zarek, then we can forget the whole thing. I'm not coming with you if—' Her voice tailed. How could she put into words what she was thinking? It would be far too embarrassing, especially if she'd got it wrong.

But Zarek was not letting her get away with it. 'If what?' His tone was serious, his face stern, and Rhianne couldn't be sure whether he was calling her bluff or whether she had actually annoyed him.

'I've just finished with one relationship, I have no intention of starting another.'

'And you think that's what I'm after?' There was indignation in his voice but a twinkle in his eyes. 'Really, Rhianne, you do me an injustice. I have a heart of gold, didn't you know that? All I'm doing is giving you the break you deserve.'

Zarek watched Rhianne's face closely, wondering whether she would believe him. God, this woman intrigued him like no one else ever had. He wanted to take her into his arms and kiss her senseless right here and now. And somehow he knew that she wouldn't stop him.

But afterwards, when the kiss ended, she would come to her senses and refuse point blank to accompany him.

He wanted her, yes—badly. But he'd never taken a woman against her will. And he wasn't about to start now. His seduction of her needed to be slow and sure.

CHAPTER FIVE

RHIANNE knew that she ought not to have been surprised that Zarek had his own private jet, but, nevertheless, she had been. After her initial shock, though, she had got used to the luxury. Zarek had busied himself with some paperwork, so she'd been able to relax and enjoy. An army of staff had pampered her and fed her, making her feel as though she was someone special, and now they had arrived on Santorini.

The heat greeted them. The sky was a hot blue, the waters of the Aegean translucent and inviting, and the white glare of the buildings made her wish that her sunglasses weren't packed in her case. Alighting from the plane felt like stepping into an oven. But in no time at all they were ushered into an air-conditioned car and whisked away from the busy little airport.

'We must go to see my mother first,' Zarek told her. 'She is expecting us.'

'Us?' queried Rhianne. 'You've told her about me?'

'I phoned her last night. She's looking forward to meeting you.'

'So she's used to your staff accompanying you?' Zarek

was such a busy man that she wouldn't put it past him to take a retinue of employees wherever he went.

'Actually, no. I've never brought any of my work-force here.'

A frown dragged Rhianne's fine brows together. If this was the case, why was he taking her to meet his mother? Why couldn't he have dropped her off at his villa and gone to see his parent alone? Surely they wouldn't want a stranger in their midst at such a critical time.

When they reached his family home—an impressive white villa near the beautiful village of Oia, overlooking a water-filled crater left by a volcanic eruption many years earlier—his mother came rushing out to greet them.

'Zarek.' She held out her arms and folded him in them. She was shorter than her son, very slender and elegantly dressed, and her dark hair bore no sign of grey. She looked like one very determined lady, thought Rhianne as she held back while mother and son embraced.

Zarek hugged her tightly and kissed the top of her head. 'You look well, Mother,' he said in English, which Rhianne guessed was for her benefit.

'Someone has to be,' she said lightly, pulling out of his embrace. 'And this is Rhianne, I presume?' Her English was good but heavily accented. 'You are very welcome here, Rhianne. Come inside both of you and I will fix you a cool drink. What was your flight like? And how is England? Is this your first visit to Santorini?'

She spoke non-stop, each sentence falling over the previous one, giving Rhianne no chance to say anything. She glanced at Zarek, watched the way his eyebrows rose and his lips turned down comically at the corners as if to say, this is my mother, this is what she's like. You'll never get a word in.

'How is your husband?' Rhianne managed to ask when the woman finally paused for breath.

'Ah, Georgios, he is not well. But he is looking forward to Zarek's visit. You too, of course, must go to see him. He was very, very happy when I told him Zarek was bringing a lady friend. Our son, he has no time for romance, you understand? He is always busy, busy, busy. I trust you will get him to change his ways. You are beautiful, Rhianne, just the sort of girl I envisaged for him.'

Swift alarm filled Rhianne's body, sparking its way through every inch of it, and she flashed a pointed glance at Zarek, suddenly guessing that he had known all along that his mother would assume they were in a relationship. It might even have been what he'd wanted her to think, though why was a mystery. Why would he want to pretend that she was his girlfriend when they'd only known each other for five minutes?

He looked completely unperturbed by the deception; in fact, he was grinning. And this infuriated Rhianne even more. How dare he put her in this position! What sort of game did he think he was playing? If it hadn't been for his father's illness, she would have lashed out there and then and told him exactly what she thought of him.

She could feel her blood boiling and her brain cells working overtime. She wouldn't mention it in front of his mother as she didn't want to upset her. She would bide her time. But if he thought she would sit back and take it all in her stride, then he was very much mistaken.

'Come and get your drinks.' His mother's voice broke into her thoughts. 'And then you must both go to see

Georgios. He is waiting impatiently. Leave your cases, Zarek. Yannis will take them up to your room.'

'We are not staying here, Mother,' he informed her quickly. 'Rhianne and I will be staying at my villa.'

His mother smiled knowingly. 'But, of course. What was I thinking? You two lovebirds will want to be on your own. And I do not blame you. But you will come to see me every day? You will visit your father?'

'Naturally,' answered Zarek. 'But I also want to show Rhianne around the island.'

It was but a short journey to the hospital. Rhianne sat quietly fuming, well aware that Zarek knew what was going on in her mind. Whether he was grateful that she was holding her tongue she didn't know, but he sure as hell needn't think that he'd got away with it. If it wasn't for the chauffeur, he'd be feeling the sharp edge of her anger right now.

Zarek was very much like his father, decided Rhianne, as they sat beside the older man's hospital bed a few minutes later. Georgios's face was pale, with lines of strain, but the similarities were strong. The shape of the face, the well-marked brows, even the same eyes. He was a gentle man who welcomed Rhianne warmly.

'I am sorry you have to see me like this,' he said. 'But it is better this way than not to see you at all. My son doesn't come home often enough; you are obviously a good influence on him.' He turned to Zarek. 'Why have you never told us about Rhianne? She is very beautiful. I have never seen hair such a rich colour. May I touch?' he asked with a faint smile.

'Of course.' Self-consciously Rhianne leaned forward. She had pinned it on top of her head for the flight, but after freshening up at Zarek's mother's house she had left it loose about her shoulders. Zarek had once said that he preferred it this way but she'd done it for quickness, most definitely not for him.

Georgios stroked her hair slowly, letting its luxurious length slide through his weak fingers. Rhianne glanced at Zarek and saw the narrowing of his eyes and a muscle pulsing in his jaw, and she knew instinctively that he wished that he was the one touching.

But she also knew that he wouldn't be content to just stroke; he'd want more from her. He'd want something she wasn't prepared to give. And if these were the sort of plans he'd had when he persuaded her to join him, then he was in for a very big surprise.

Eventually Georgios's eyes closed, and Zarek indicated that they should leave. This time the car took them towards his villa. The streets of Oia were on many different levels, running like mazes between whitewashed cottages with sunny verandas; the blue domes of the churches provided a startling contrast.

Zarek's villa was on the opposite side of the village to his parents' house, for which Rhianne was grateful because she had envisaged his mother calling often to see them. Again, it was high on the cliff-side with spectacular views over the caldera and the tip of the volcano, which now formed an island.

The views were magnificent but the villa even more so. Far too big not to be used on a regular basis. Biding her time, still waiting for the right moment before she said anything, Rhianne allowed Zarek to give her a tour of the house.

On the ground floor was the kitchen, plus several dining and living areas, with doors leading out to a shady courtyard. Beyond that was an impressive swimming pool. Each room was minimally furnished with dark furniture and wall hangings but everything was of the highest quality. It took Rhianne's breath away.

Upstairs was a stunning master bedroom with a high-domed ceiling and an en-suite bathroom with its own jacuzzi as well as a separate shower. Her jaw dropped when she saw it. 'If I had a place like this, I'd want to live here all the time.'

'I used to,' he answered with a wry smile, 'until we opened the UK branch. And I fully intend coming back.'

Along the corridor were several smaller bedrooms, each with their own en suite shower room, and Rhianne wondered which one would be hers—until they reached the last one, which again took her breath away. It was oversized and magnificently furnished, with an archway leading through to a dressing room. Beyond that was the bathroom where again only the highest quality fittings had been used.

Another door led through to a large terrace where trailing bougainvillea offered something restful to feast her eyes on. She took a deep breath. 'This is lovely. And just look at the views.'

But when she turned, Zarek was studying her instead. Was that hunger she saw? The brown of his irises were flecked with gold, something she had never noticed before, and the awful thing was that she couldn't drag her eyes away.

She stood there for a full thirty seconds, tingles of fear rippling through her veins, and it was Zarek himself who finally spoke. 'So which room is it to be?' he asked quietly.

Rhianne came to her senses, shaking her head, squashing her unbidden thoughts. 'I don't care which room I sleep in,' she retorted, her eyes flashing suppressed anger. 'What I want to know is why you didn't correct your mother? Why did you let her think that we were—lovers.' The last word choked from her throat like a splinter being drawn from a festering wound.

'How could I disillusion her?' he asked innocently.

'You could have told her the truth in the first place.' Rhianne's eyes blazed a brilliant blue. 'You must have known what conclusion she would draw. You've made my position untenable. What is it that you're expecting me to do? Pretend to be the girl you're in love with? I'm sorry, but if that's the case then I might as well head home straight away because I'm not going along with that lie. Not at all. Never. Not under any circumstances.'

She stood her ground, glaring into Zarek's dark eyes which had narrowed dangerously.

'And if your father wasn't so ill, I'd insist that you tell them exactly what the position is between us.'

'And that is?' asked Zarek slowly.

Rhianne shook her head. 'You're unbelievable. You really think you can get away with this, don't you?'

'And you think a little mild deceit is worth all this rage?' he enquired.

The fact that he wasn't raising his voice, that he was treating the whole issue as if it meant nothing, caused Rhianne to heighten her defences.

'Mild?' she echoed loudly. 'I don't call being lied about mild. It's an unforgivable offence.'

'I didn't lie.'

'Of course not.' Sarcasm dripped from her voice like venom from a snake. 'But neither did you put your mother right.'

'You haven't told me which bedroom you're taking.'

Rhianne could have slapped him. Didn't he care what he was putting her through? Did he think it was funny? Did he think she'd be able to walk away unscathed? She drew in a deep, unsteady breath and glared at him with as much ice in her eyes as she could manage. 'You tell me. I simply couldn't care less. All I want to do is get back home to England.'

'Then you shall have this one,' he said. 'And when you've finished unpacking, you'll find me downstairs.'

Zarek smiled to himself as he left her. Rhianne's anger was healthy, and expected. And she would, hopefully, get over his little deception.

There had been times recently when her eyes had given her away. They had alternated between fear and desire. Not fear of him, but of her own feelings. And the desire—well, he knew that there were times when she had wondered what it would be like to be kissed by him.

Not the sort of kiss he had given her the day she'd collected her belongings, though even then he'd been aware that she'd felt something, but a real kiss. A lover's kiss. Otherwise why would she have reacted so wildly? It was a defence mechanism that had kicked in. Fear of the unknown. Fear of letting go again after she'd been so badly hurt.

Hopefully, it wouldn't be long before he got her to change her mind. This place was conducive to romance. He could almost imagine the seduction scene in his mind. One of Santorini's soft scented nights, a faint breeze stirring her amazing hair as they sat outside with after-dinner drinks. Rhianne relaxed and beautiful, heady with the new sights and sounds all around them.

It would take but a soft touch, a gentle word, eyes full of promise, to have her falling into his arms. He would feather kisses across her face—her eyes, her nose, her lips. He would become more daring with each second that passed until finally she gave in and kissed him back, when a whole frenzy of emotions would be released.

When Rhianne eventually came back downstairs, having changed into a short white skirt and a black camisole top, his heart gunned at an alarming rate. She looked younger and dangerously beautiful. Her magnificent hair was tied up on the top of her head, the resulting ponytail swinging as she walked.

It was silly, but he'd been jealous of his father when he'd asked to touch Rhianne's hair. The times he'd wanted to do it himself but hadn't dared ask for fear of offending her! What a sly old man his father was. Zarek had never really considered it before, it wasn't the sort of thing you thought about your parent, but he must have been a real ladies' man in his time. Perhaps the feelings never went away!

Actually, he'd like to think that when he was an older man himself, when he was married with children, maybe even grandchildren, that his feelings for his wife would never lessen. That to touch her, or even look at her, would still result in the same leaping of his senses.

'All done?' he asked, forcing himself to sound casual, when in fact he wanted to implement the seduction scene he had been planning in his mind.

Rhianne nodded.

'Then let's sit outside. It's shady in the courtyard under the old olive tree. It's one of my favourite spots. I'll get Spiros to bring us a bottle of wine. I could do with a drink before dinner, as I'm sure you can too.'

And then who knew what might happen? Maybe his dreams would come true…

Rhianne hadn't wanted to join him; she had wanted to stay in her room, her anger and resentment simmering. But she had realised how immature this would make her seem. She had hung away her clothes as slowly as she dared, putting off the moment when she had to face him again.

The real truth was that Zarek excited her like no other man ever had. And it scared her to death. She wanted to remain angry with him, and yet one look into those brown eyes, which seemed to have turned golden beneath the heat of the sun, made everything inside her melt.

After her disastrous relationship with Angus she had told herself she was done with men—for all time. Why, then, had she let Zarek slip beneath her guard? And how could she build it up again?

Every time she glanced at him his eyes were on her, and even though she tried to ignore the way her senses leapt, even though she attempted to hang on to the shreds of her anger, even though she endeavoured not to look at him, it was impossible. It was as though an invisible string kept pulling her gaze in his direction.

Their wine arrived, and Zarek waved Spiros away, filling her glass himself. 'I'd forgotten how magical this place is,' he said softly, his fingers touching hers as he handed her the drink.

Magical? Wasn't that a strange word for him to be using? It was magnificent, yes, but magical? Was he implying that this place could cast a spell over her? Was he hoping for more from her than she was prepared to give? Did he want to turn their *faux* relationship into reality?

She faced a big dilemma and needed to not only guard against Zarek—but her own feelings too.

Thankfully, over dinner Zarek defused the situation by talking non-stop about his childhood, about his younger brother, Christos, who, he declared, was nothing like himself. 'He has no get up and go,' he claimed derisively. 'Christos relies too heavily on other people.'

'Does he live here? Will I meet him?' asked Rhianne.

Zarek's eyes flashed. 'I doubt it. He married a girl from the mainland and lives there now. But he's not averse to sponging off my parents. I'm not even sure what he does for a living any more, if anything. He's work-shy I'm afraid.'

'How can two brothers be so different?' she mused. 'I used to long to have a sister. I imagined that we'd be very close and very alike in our tastes. But it wasn't to be.'

'Do you want children of your own?' There was an odd inflection in his voice that made Rhianne look at him sharply.

'Do you?'

For a moment there was silence between them. Rhianne took a sip of her wine and waited for his answer. A light breeze rustled the leaves on the olive tree. She didn't know why, but she felt that his answer to her casual question was important.

Finally, he spoke. 'As I've never considered marriage an option, I guess I've never thought about it.'

'But now that you have—thought about it, I mean?' Heaven forbid that he should think she was asking him about the marriage option.

'If they turned out like Christos, definitely no, I wouldn't want any. But if I had a daughter who looked like you—well, I'd want to lock up every eligible young man in the neighbourhood. Has anyone ever told you how beautiful you are, Rhianne?'

How had the conversation got round to her? Rhianne felt herself blushing furiously, something she hadn't done since she was a young girl. 'You flatter me,' she said, trying her hardest to keep her tone light and inconsequential. 'Do you say that to all the girls?'

An eyebrow lifted, and he appeared to be considering her question. Then he smiled, a wicked smile that suggested he might be teasing; on the other hand he could be deadly serious.

'You know what it is that I find attractive about you, Rhianne? Your hair. Sometimes it glows red like in a Titian painting. At other times it's so dark as to be almost sable. Do you know I was jealous of my father touching it? The times I've wanted to do exactly the same thing but been too scared.'

Zarek scared? She didn't believe that for one second. What she did believe was that if he dared to run his fingers through her hair, it would be the beginning of something more. She was well aware how thick and luxurious it was, and she'd always been complimented on it. Not that she ever consciously thought about it herself, but if Zarek touched it, if he let its silky length fall through his fingers like a curtain, if he took it in his hands and pulled her face close to his, then she would be lost.

Here in this place that he had declared magical, a spell would be woven over her, and every inhibition she'd ever had would be lifted by the breeze and floated away over the sea.

And she was being fanciful!

'I can't believe that you'd be scared of anything,

Zarek.' Bravely she steadied her eyes on his face, daring him to refute it.

'You'd be surprised, Rhianne. Some things are too good to spoil.'

CHAPTER SIX

ZAREK watched Rhianne over the breakfast table. He hadn't enjoyed sleeping in separate rooms at different ends of the villa. He'd lain awake half the night trying to imagine what it would be like to have her lying beside him, to feel her soft body against his, to inhale the seductive womanly smell of her. Even thinking about it now tightened his muscles, made him clamp down on urges that would give him away.

Last night they'd sat and talked long into the night, and he had felt an impulse to bed her like none he had ever felt before. But Rhianne had remained highly defensive, still unhappy about the way he had deceived his parents, and he hadn't dared force the issue so early in their relationship.

This morning she wore a blue strappy dress that reflected the colour of her eyes. It was made of some thin fabric that clung slavishly to her breasts, and the second she'd joined him for breakfast his breath had caught in his throat.

It didn't look as though she was wearing a bra underneath, and he'd looked forward to spending the whole day with her, visualising her gently rounded breasts free of any restrictions. His fingers ached to touch, to feel her delectable shape, and he'd had problems stopping his mouth from going dry.

But when he suggested she accompany him to the hospital, Rhianne shook her head vigorously. 'I told you yesterday I'd be happy here on my own. I need time to unwind.'

He knew it was an excuse. She was still angry with him. And, in reality, he couldn't blame her, but, hell, pretending that she was his girlfriend had seemed a good idea at the time. 'Are you positive you won't come? I don't like the thought of leaving you here on your own,' he suggested, lowering his voice persuasively.

Rhianne's blue eyes boldly met his. 'You really think I'd be comfortable facing your parents again under the circumstances? This is *your* mercy visit, not mine.'

'They will think it strange if you don't accompany me.' He wasn't afraid to use emotional blackmail.

But still Rhianne shook her head. She did not want to see Zarek's parents; she did not want his mother to gush over her in the opinion that she was her son's chosen one. It was wrong. He should have put her right straight away. 'Go visit your father, talk to your mother, I will stay here,' she said resolutely. 'And then, if you still want to, we will go out together.'

'Do you promise?' he enquired, his dark eyes filled with doubt.

In the distance Rhianne could hear the faint jingle of bells from the mules ferrying goods from the docks up to the villages, and she heard gulls mewing as they circled far below, looking for fish. She tried to concentrate on these sounds instead of answering Zarek, but soon realised that she could remain silent no longer.

'I promise,' she said huskily.

Zarek tried again. 'My parents will be disappointed.'

'Tell them I insisted. Tell them that I thought you should spend time on your own with them. Better still, tell them the truth, Zarek,' she finished firmly.

He closed his eyes, and she knew that he wouldn't. He preferred the misunderstanding. Perhaps his mother was keen for him to settle down. Perhaps it was for his own peace of mind that he allowed the illusion.

The villa felt empty when he had gone. Rhianne had thought she would enjoy being here by herself, but in fact she felt isolated and lonely. It was filled with Zarek's personality. Even though he'd lived in London for a long time his presence here was dominant.

She wandered from room to room, running her fingers over the dark pieces of furniture, peering at paintings of local scenes, wondering who had painted them. She even ventured into his bedroom, with its unusual domed ceiling, feasting her eyes on his bed.

The maid had straightened the covers, and there was nothing to suggest that Zarek had spent the night here. Alone! Her heart did a little wobble. What would it be like, she wondered, to share the bed with him? To feel his body against her? To be kissed by him, to be touched, to be teased, to be brought to vibrant life?

God, where had those thoughts come from? It was so unlike her. In all her years she had never had such thoughts. Shaking her head, Rhianne wandered through to the magnificent en suite.

Here were Zarek's toiletries, lined up on a glass shelf in soldierly fashion. The musky smell of his cologne lingered in the air, the same one that he'd used in London, she realised. She guessed it was a subconscious thing, and she couldn't help wondering whether there was anything else she had unknowingly noticed about him.

He was getting through to her in a way she had never envisaged. She ought to be in the depths of despair having been let down so badly by Angus, she ought to still be angry with Zarek for misleading his parents, and yet her thoughts constantly turned to him.

Why, was the question she kept asking herself.

'I don't believe you're telling me this.' Zarek stared at his father in disbelief, his dark eyes passionately angry. 'You're saying that if I'm not married when you—' he choked on the words '—when you die, that the business will go to Christos?'

'That is correct, my son. It is an unfortunate state of affairs, but that is how it is.'

'But Christos would run it into the ground,' declared Zarek fiercely, his voice filling the hospital room. 'He has no business sense. He will spend, spend, spend. You know what he is like.'

'I do indeed,' answered his father sadly. 'But there is not a thing I can do about it. My great grandfather put the condition into his will because he felt that marriage made a man more stable. Failing that, it would pass to his second son, and so on down the line. Each generation has honoured his wish. It is now my turn to do the same. Do not think I am taking this lightly; I have consulted lawyers many times, and it is always the same. It is an airtight condition; there is no getting out of it.'

'There must be a way,' declared Zarek heatedly. 'I'll look into it. There has to be a loophole. It's ridiculous.'

'Exactly what I thought, but believe me I have tried.'

Not hard enough, thought Zarek. The very thought of Christos inheriting made his head spin. He'd spent years running the business, increasing it in value, opening new offices. He couldn't let it go. *He couldn't!*

'Why didn't you tell me sooner?' he demanded, getting to his feet and pacing the room.

'Because, my son, I didn't want you getting wedded solely for the sake of the business. It would be disastrous. I want you to be as happily married as I am.'

'So you thought you'd wait until…near the end—and then drop the bombshell on me?' Zarek questioned loudly and angrily, sinking back into his chair.

'Nothing of the sort,' declared the older man, sitting up much straighter, his weary eyes suddenly fierce. 'I'm not going yet, don't worry about that. But surely you must guess the reason I've told you now. Your beautiful friend, Rhianne. It did my heart good to see that you've finally found a woman to love.'

'But—Father, I—'

'Don't say anything. Don't tell me it's too soon, that you haven't been going out long. I know love when I see it. Why else would you have brought her to see us? She is perfect for you, Zarek. Your mother and I, we are very happy.'

Zarek wanted to hotly deny feeling anything but lust for the beautiful Rhianne, but his father's hand was on his, his eyes trusting now, and an idea began to form.

When Zarek returned home, he found Rhianne sitting reading in the shady courtyard. While she was still unaware of his presence, he was able to quietly observe her. She still wore the blue sundress, a matching band holding her hair back from her face. Thick dark lashes fringed her stunning eyes, and a faint smile played about her infinitely kissable lips.

Her eyes swivelled in his direction, and she smiled. A faintly guarded smile; nevertheless, it did treacherous things to his body. 'I didn't expect you back this soon,' she said softly. 'How's your father?'

'Much the same. No worse, no better.' He walked over to her and looked down. 'He asked why you didn't accompany me.'

Whether it was because Rhianne was here, in his home country, looking for all the world as though she belonged, he didn't know, but he had the strongest urge yet to haul her to her feet and kiss her soundly. He didn't, of course. He fought the feeling with every ounce of strength he could muster. There was no sense in frightening her away before he'd put his plan into action.

'What did you tell him?'

'That you thought it was a son's duty to visit his father alone.'

Rhianne's lovely eyes widened in denial.

'Actually, no, I didn't,' he responded with a grin, 'but he did ask where you were. And he enquired after your well-being. He likes you, Rhianne.'

'He hardly knows me.'

'I didn't know you when I offered the job. It was a good choice, though. You proved yourself to be a good worker.'

'And now you're rewarding me with a holiday. I know. I've heard it all before,' she said with exaggerated boredom.

'And I'll carry on saying it. But it's my reward too. It's rare I take holidays these days, and I intend, if you will allow me, to enjoy it. Come—' he held out his hand '—let me show you my beautiful island.'

Rhianne felt her heart lurch as she let Zarek pull her to her feet, and the whole day flew by in a blur of new sights and sounds. He took her to secret coves, and a tiny hidden restaurant. It was like being in a world of their own, a world where fun and relaxation was the order of the day.

They were laughing at some silly joke he'd made when they got back to his villa, and when Rhianne stumbled down one of the steps he was quick to catch her. The smiles were wiped off their faces as their eyes made contact, and, in less time than it took to draw breath, Zarek's mouth claimed hers.

Rhianne didn't stop him. She couldn't. She had known all day long that it would happen. There had been a rapport between them, an extra awareness, a special sensitivity, and something deep down inside her had cried out for his kisses.

In fact, it was a relief when he did kiss her because it released the tension and she was able to breathe more easily. Sliding her hands behind his neck, she returned his kiss with a passion that shocked her. Never had she kissed a man so deeply before, never had she felt electrical impulses zizz through her veins. It was as though she'd touched a live wire.

'Oh, Zarek!' The words were dragged from her lips as they paused for breath.

'Oh, Zarek, what?' he asked softly, his mouth still against hers.

She could taste his clean breath, feel the tautness in his limbs, and even more telling was the extent of his arousal. 'What are you doing to me?'

His smile was slow and sensual. 'The same as you are doing to me.' He punctuated each word with more tiny kisses at the corners of her mouth.

'But I didn't ask for any of this, we're not supposed to be—'

'Kissing? Exciting each other? Having fun? Life's too short, Rhianne, not to take advantage of every situation.'

'You mean that you're taking advantage of me?' she asked with mock indignation. She knew that he wasn't; she was a willing participant—amazingly so. She was shocking even herself by her openness.

'What do you think?'

'I think it's time we went indoors and showered off the dust of the day.'

'Good idea, Rhianne. And after the shower, the jacuzzi. It's simply begging to be used.'

There was no escape, not that she wanted any. She liked the feelings he generated. So long as he didn't expect too much of her then she was prepared to go along with his game. He was actually making her feel good about herself again, and for that she was grateful.

But as she pulled on a swimsuit following her shower, Rhianne began to feel nervous. Perhaps it wasn't such a good idea sharing the jacuzzi. It would be far more intimate than sitting in his car, or exploring the island. It might even lead to something that she wasn't ready for. Even as the thought occurred to her, Zarek came to find out what was taking her so long.

All he wore was a pair of black close-fitting shorts, and she couldn't help sucking in a breath at the sight of his hard-muscled body. It was long and lean with a scattering of dark hairs on his chest. His hips were slim and his legs powerful.

'I thought you'd changed your mind,' he said easily, 'but I see that you're ready.'

Rhianne nodded, unable to speak. The breath had been whisked from her throat at the sight of him. He was more male than she had imagined, and deeply, darkly dangerous.

She followed him along the corridor, unable to take her eyes off him. There was not an ounce of superfluous fat anywhere. His olive skin was smooth and toned, his limbs powerful, and she couldn't help but wonder what it would be like to be held against that naked body, to feel the power for herself.

They reached his bedroom, and it felt faintly indecent to be walking through it—even though she'd taken that inquisitive look this morning—and when they reached his bathroom she stood for a few seconds before climbing into the hot tub.

Actually, it was heaven. The jets of water soon relaxed her tense muscles, and Zarek's non-stop conversation had her in fits of laughter. But then, without warning, his face became serious. 'My father told me the terms of his will this morning.'

And he was telling her for what reason? Rhianne couldn't help feeling puzzled. 'Judging by your expression, you're not impressed. But you shouldn't discuss it with me. This should be private between you and your family.'

'One would think so,' he agreed. 'But it's not that simple.' He rubbed his fingers over his brow as he spoke, and Rhianne itched to take them, to touch her lips to them, to still his movement.

'I don't see how I can help. Really, Zarek, I'd feel embarrassed if you disclosed any details.'

'But that's the point. You can help.' There was raw pain

in his eyes now, something Rhianne had never seen before. He was such a big, capable man that she couldn't imagine anything hurting him.

'How?' Her question was little more than a whisper. Did she want to do this? Did she want to get involved in something concerning his family when she was only just beginning to get over the trauma of her own problems?

'By marrying me.'

Whatever Rhianne had expected Zarek to say it had been nothing like this. For a few seconds she stopped breathing, did nothing except stare at him, her blue eyes wide and fixed. Outside a pair of birds squabbled. In the room her pulses threatened to jump clear through her skin. 'Did I hear you correctly?' And was that her speaking, was that strangled, tiny voice really her own?

Zarek merely nodded, as though he too found it diffi-cult to voice his thoughts. Beneath his tan he was pale, and his hands, spread out on either side of him, clutched the side of the tub as though he was afraid of being dragged under.

'But why?' Her faint whisper barely reached above the sound of the throbbing water.

'It's complicated.'

'It sure sounds it.' Complicated didn't even begin to describe her fear.

'It goes back to an iron-clad condition my great grandfather—the one who started the family business— put in his will.'

'He said you had to marry Rhianne Pickering?' Rhianne tried to make light of the situation, but her words merely sounded stupid.

'Each eldest son has to be married before he can inherit.'

'So?' she questioned, still not sure that she understood what he was saying.

'If he's not, it's the second eldest and so on.'

'Then there isn't a problem, surely, not with Christos being married?'

Zarek's eyes flashed angrily. 'Christos couldn't run the business if his life depended on it. He'd spend the profit rather than earn it.'

'So you're telling me that if you're not married when your father dies, then everything goes to him. And you think that would be the end of the business?'

He nodded. 'I'm sure of it.'

'And you've only just been told this?' Her brows rose dramatically. 'Why?'

'Because my parents didn't want me to marry purely for the sake of the business. They want me to marry for love.'

The full import of what he was saying began to sink in.

'And they think that you and I—are…'

Zarek nodded.

CHAPTER SEVEN

RHIANNE couldn't believe that Zarek was actually asking her to marry him. Surely he must know what her answer would be? Heavens, she was still getting over Angus's betrayal. Marriage was out of the question for many years to come.

If ever!

He had an incredible nerve. Did he really think she would agree? How could she marry a man she hardly knew? And Zarek certainly wasn't the type to enjoy a marriage without sex—even if it was to save the company. He would want more from her, far more than she was prepared to give. He would want a proper relationship, and even though her feelings had stirred when he had kissed her—dangerous feelings—she had no intention whatsoever of committing herself to him.

How long she sat in the bubbling waters of the Jacuzzi, tossing Zarek's question round and round in her mind, Rhianne did not know. It felt like hours, though in all probability it was only minutes, maybe even seconds.

Did he really know what he was asking? How impossible it would be for her? Maybe when he'd had time for everything to sink in he would think differently. He'd realise that it was an unfair proposition. He would know that she couldn't possibly do it.

His voice cut into her thoughts, caused her eyes to swiftly turn in his direction. Every muscle in his face was set and hard; even his eyes looked as though they had turned to stone. 'It's my life we're talking about. If you refuse, you'll be crumbling everything to ashes beneath my feet.'

Rhianne drew in a long, slow breath through her nose; there was a tangible silence between them. The very air had stilled as though it too was waiting to hear what her answer would be.

'I'll think about it,' she said softly, not wanting to hurt him any more at this moment, but confident that her answer would be no. She couldn't marry a man she hardly knew. For whatever reason. It would be disastrous. Heavens, she'd known Angus for years before she'd agreed to become his wife. And even then events had proved that she hadn't known him as well as she'd thought!

She was well aware of the fact that the business meant everything to Zarek, and his fear that he might lose it was very real. But was his brother really as bad as he made out? Would the business really go down? It could be that the rivalry between them had nothing to do with the company. It could be some private feud of which she knew nothing.

'I'd like to meet Christos before I make a decision,' she said firmly, daring to meet his eyes, shocked by the dullness in them. Zarek truly believed that she was his only hope. He was certain that Christos would ruin everything he'd worked for. But she couldn't take his word for it, she needed to find out for herself.

'I assure you there's no point,' he declared. 'Christos

is a wastrel. He always has been and always will be. Ask my father.'

'I don't want to ask your father,' declared Rhianne fiercely, her blue eyes blazing into his now. 'I want to find out for myself.'

'You do realise that you're my only hope?'

Zarek wanted to take her into his arms and kiss her senseless, he wanted to make her his in every sense of the word so that she wouldn't even think about refusing him. Rhianne was undoubtedly struggling with her conscience. She'd only just escaped one unwise marriage, why should she even think about entering another?

Somehow he had to persuade her. It wasn't as if there was no spark between them. There was. Most definitely. Even if she denied it. Marriage to Rhianne would be no hardship. In fact, it would be a pleasure. Whether it would work out long term was another question, but not one he intended to think about now.

There was nothing in the will to say that a divorce somewhere down the line would affect his inheritance. And he would make certain that she didn't lose out. Was this why she was hesitating, wondering what would become of her at the end of it all?

'I wouldn't tie you to a loveless marriage for the rest of your life, Rhianne,' he said carefully. 'And I'd definitely make it worth your while. You'd end up a very rich woman.'

'You make it sound so simple,' she said, her eyes wide and shadowed. And very, very beautiful. He had never seen them look so luminous or so large. He cursed himself for making the suggestion so quickly. He should have forewarned her, he should have explained the situation first so that she knew the predicament he was in. If she'd felt sorry for him, she might have been more amenable to his suggestion.

Now she clearly felt that he was exaggerating. She wanted to meet his brother, for goodness' sake, find out for herself what he was like. It would all take time, and time wasn't something he had a lot of. He had never seen his father look so ill as he had this morning. He'd put on a pretence, but his sallow face and dull eyes had given him away.

Zarek didn't want to wait for her decision. He didn't want to give her time to think about it in case she turned and ran. He needed an answer now. A commitment now. Otherwise, all the hard work he'd put into building up the business had been for nothing.

And he knew who'd jump in at the kill if Christos decided to sell the business rather than go to the trouble of trying to run it. Their bitterest competitor and enemy, Theron Papadakis.

Zarek had gone to school with Theron; they'd been rivals even then. And over the years Theron had done all he could to poach Zarek's customers. Fortunately, they had remained loyal to Zarek, and the company had gone from strength to strength. It would be the deepest humiliation if it fell into his enemy's hands now.

Somehow he had to persuade Rhianne to say yes.

'I realise this is all very sudden,' he said, smiling softly, keeping his voice soft too, though he had no idea how he managed it when inside he was burning with despair, 'but it's a matter of the utmost urgency. My father doesn't have long to live.' He hadn't actually been told this, but his parent had deteriorated rapidly since his last visit, and he knew now why his mother had asked him to come.

'Then you'd better fix a meeting with your brother as soon as you can,' she declared. The more he pushed her the more determined she was to dig her heels in. Without another word, she climbed out of the hot tub and headed back to her room.

With the door firmly closed behind her, Rhianne drew in several deep steadying breaths. Zarek's proposal had come out of the blue, and she felt disturbed by it. He'd never been more serious in his life, she could tell that. He was deeply worried about the business and saw her as his only saviour.

Didn't he realise how much he was asking of her, though? He'd made it sound as though he was asking her for a date. Not a lifelong commitment. Why he ever thought she would agree Rhianne had no idea. And she hoped against hope that his brother would turn out to be a decent guy.

Family feuds always dragged up deep resentment. If Zarek's hostility towards Christos was caused by something else, then it would be up to him to resolve it. Not drag her into the mire. He was being most unfair, and she wished, not for the first time, that she had never come out here with him.

After another shower Rhianne threw herself down on the bed. It was almost time for bed anyway, and she had no wish to talk to Zarek again. She'd said all she wanted to say; it was up to him now.

She half expected him to come tapping on the door, but it grew dark and she fell asleep, not waking again until the early hours of the morning.

When she went down for breakfast, Zarek was missing. Spiros informed her that he'd gone out early, and he had no idea when he would be back.

So Rhianne ate breakfast alone, not really hungry, merely nibbling on the fresh bread that had appeared on the table. Drinking cup after cup of black coffee instead. Her thoughts were deep. She had dreamt about being married to Zarek, resenting him for forcing her into it and totally refusing to share his bed. Which angered him because he couldn't see the point of marriage without sex.

When he came back he didn't look in the best of moods, and Rhianne was almost afraid to ask him what was wrong. 'Is it your father?' she suggested tentatively. 'Is he worse?' Oh, God, what if he died and Zarek's worst fears were realised? It would be her fault.

'I've been in touch with Christos,' he told her tersely.

'You've said I want to see him?'

'Of course not. I told him how ill Father is. I've said he should get over here.'

'And is he coming?'

Zarek lifted his broad shoulders, letting them drop again slowly. 'Time will tell.'

Nevertheless, Rhianne couldn't get it out of her head that Zarek might be exaggerating. Surely his brother wasn't quite such the cold callous man he was painting? He could be a perfect gentleman. Their enmity could be nothing more than a conflict of opinion. It wasn't unknown for two brothers to hate each other's guts, but it didn't mean that one of them wasn't capable of running a business.

'Tell me more about him,' she said. I always wanted a brother, someone older, someone I could look up to.'

'Christos would most definitely not have fitted that bill.' Zarek gave a derogatory snort, a flash of fire in his eyes. 'He never looked up to me. He was a mummy's boy.

I think he objected to having an older brother; he wanted all of her attention. Admittedly, he was a sickly child and needed extra care, but did he play on it!'

'I'm sorry,' said Rhianne softly. 'That's not how it should be.'

'In a perfect world,' he snorted.

'It's a shame you two don't get on,' she said softly, reaching out to touch his hand across the table.

'Tell me about it,' he answered crisply. 'If Christos was a different man, and we ran the company together, there'd be no stopping us.'

'It seems to me that you've done pretty well by yourself.' He nodded. 'I'm satisfied.'

'But if Christos takes over…'

Zarek's nostrils flared. 'It doesn't bear thinking about.'

Rhianne shivered at the dark tones in his voice. Nevertheless, she still felt the need to meet Christos herself.

It happened sooner than she expected. A few hours later Zarek took a phone call from his brother to say that he was at the hospital. 'We're meeting up at my mother's house,' he told Rhianne tersely. 'Come, we'll go now.'

'I'd rather meet him here,' she prevaricated. The very thought of facing Zarek's mother again, of seeing the happiness in her eyes that her eldest son had found the woman he wanted to marry, made her uneasy.

'It can't be done. I would not allow him into my house. It might sound hard to you, Rhianne, but you don't know him.'

How could anyone be that awful, she thought. How could you hate your own brother so much? But when she met Christos two hours later she saw for herself why.

Christos looked nothing like Zarek. He was tall, yes,

but his body carried a lot of excess weight—as though he enjoyed the high life without too much thought about what it was doing to him. Nor did he attempt to hide how much he despised his older brother.

'Who is this?' he asked sneeringly when he saw Rhianne. 'Don't tell me you've finally found someone to put up with all the long hours that you work? Does she know what she's letting herself in for?'

And, without waiting for Zarek to answer, he turned to Rhianne. 'There'll be no fun for you with my brother,' he declared. 'No life for you. He's in love with his job. You'll come a poor second best.'

'I think I should be the judge of that,' she said, lifting her chin as her hackles rose.

From the moment the two men met she had seen antagonism flare. They didn't even try to hide it from their mother. And later, when Rhianne heard Christos asking his mother for money, she knew that everything Zarek had said was true.

She felt deeply sorry for him and could see now why he feared for the business if it ever fell into Christos's hands.

It was a very uncomfortable two hours before Zarek finally announced that they were leaving.

'So soon?' asked his mother.

'Rhianne and I have things to do,' he answered. 'I'll see you tomorrow.' He kissed her fondly but he didn't even look at his brother.

Neither of them spoke until they were in the car and on their way back to his villa. She could see from the way Zarek's knuckles gleamed white as he gripped the wheel how angry he was, how much he had hated forcing Christos to come over and prove his point.

'I hope now you believe me,' he growled fiercely, flashing her a swift, brutal glance.

'I'm sorry,' replied Rhianne, feeling as if he had kicked her. 'I should have believed you; it would have saved all this embarrassment.'

'I think Christos did a very good job of proving to you what a bastard he is?'

Rhianne nodded uncomfortably.

'Perhaps now you'll be prepared to consider my offer? It's my only hope—you are aware of that?'

How could she not be? It had been on her mind since he had mentioned it yesterday.

Perhaps if they agreed to a marriage on paper only then it wouldn't be so bad. She enjoyed Zarek's company, and it would certainly give her security. It might even be the only way she ever found happiness with a man, because how could she trust anyone after the way Angus had behaved, after the way her father had treated her mother? She had even begun to wonder whether there was any man in the world who remained true to one woman for the whole of his life.

Zarek's parents excluded. Though they were the exception rather than the norm. She sensed that if Zarek gave his word that would be it. She wouldn't need to fear that he would renege on their deal. She could settle down without fear that he would try to persuade her into a more personal relationship.

Couldn't she?

An element of doubt still lay in her mind. Zarek was a healthy male with a healthy male appetite, and she didn't want him to make promises that he couldn't keep. Dared she trust him?

What she had to do, if she agreed to his suggestion, was make sure that he understood the rules of the game. Otherwise it was a definite no. Rhianne was giving her body to no man—not unless she loved him truly and deeply and he returned those very same feelings.

This marriage was not about love, it was about saving a very successful company. It was a business proposition—and she was going to get well paid for it at the end of the day. If they made rules and stuck by them then she would be foolish to turn down what could prove to be a very lucrative agreement.

Rhianne didn't answer Zarek's question. The rest of the journey was accomplished in silence, each deep in their own thoughts. Not until they had reached his villa, and he had garaged the car, did he speak of it again.

Spiros brought wine to them outside where they sat silently in the courtyard, and after they had taken a few sips Zarek once more asked the inevitable question. 'You've had time to think about it, you've seen for yourself that I was speaking the truth about my brother, do you want the downfall of Diakos Holdings to be on your conscience?'

'That's not fair,' she retorted immediately, her eyes sparking blue flashes. 'That's blackmail.'

'I don't know how else to ask you.'

'Persuasion usually works.'

Zarek's eyes narrowed. And after a few seconds he leaned closer towards her. Rhianne felt his soft, clean breath on her face and realised what sort of persuasion he thought she had meant. Instantly she fended him off with her hands, not exactly touching him, but making sure that he knew her defences were up.

'I'll tell you the decision I've reached,' she said quietly, trying to ignore the way her body had reacted to his nearness. She really would have to make the rules very clear if she wanted any peace of mind.

Zarek immediately sat back in his chair and folded his arms. His dark eyes never left her face, scrutinising every tiny movement: the way she nervously sank her teeth into her lower lip, the way she tried to avert her eyes from his gaze, how her breathing grew that little bit quicker.

'I'll agree to marry you, but with certain conditions.'

His well-shaped brows rose, and Rhianne knew that he was already wondering whether he would like what she had to say. She knew in her own mind that he wouldn't. Zarek would expect nothing less than a normal marriage, with her in bed beside him every night.

It couldn't be done. All her life she'd been waiting for Mr Right. Zarek wasn't that person. She hardly knew him. He'd almost run her over and then made amends by offering her a job. But if he thought it gave him some prior claim on her body then he was deeply mistaken.

'Our marriage would be in name only,' she said quietly. 'A pure business deal. Nothing more, nothing less.' She kept her eyes steady on his, trying to judge his reaction, but not by the flicker of an eyelash did he give anything away. He remained still and silent, waiting for her to continue.

'We would sleep in separate rooms, and you would not even attempt to kiss me. Whether we remain here or in England it makes no difference. And at the end of it all, when I get my freedom, I shall expect you to let me go and not bother me again.'

Even as she said these words Rhianne knew that she sounded hard and callous. But she had to safeguard herself;

she couldn't go through with the marriage otherwise. She hadn't remained a virgin for all these years to lose it to some man who wanted to save his family business.

No matter that he was stunningly handsome with eyes that should never be allowed to look at a woman as though he wanted to ravish her right there and then. It was going to be hard to ignore his sexuality, she was well aware of that, but it was what she had to do.

It would be cruel of her not to help. Having got to know Zarek, discovering for herself that he was a kind, fair man, it was the least she could do.

So long as he understood the rules!

'You drive a hard bargain, Rhianne. Have you any idea how utterly gorgeous you are?'

Rhianne shrugged. 'I've never looked at myself in that light.'

'Do you know how hard you're making this for me?'

'It depends how badly you want my help. As I see it, you have no choice.'

Zarek drew in a deep, unsteady breath, closing his eyes for a few seconds, and when he looked at her again she saw that relief had taken the place of fear. He held out his hand. 'We have a deal.'

But when she took it he pulled her hard against him, sealing their deal with a kiss. A full on kiss that went against everything she'd just said. And yet before she could fight him, before she could drag her mouth away and protest, he let her go.

But not before she had felt the full impact of his kiss.

It had ripped through her body with lightning speed, it had set off a chain reaction, each pulse in turn stammering to make itself felt. He had fed new life into her veins, and for one crazy second she had wanted the kiss to continue. Just for one second, that was all, and now she was left staring in horror into his face.

'You shouldn't have done that.'

'I was sealing our bargain.'

'We could have shaken hands.' The moment the words left her lips she realised how ludicrous they sounded. Admittedly, it was a business deal, but shaking hands would surely have been better when emotions were running high!

'It's a pity you don't want me to kiss you any more, Rhianne, because you're a very kissable person.'

'I hope you're not going to renege on our deal?' Rhianne's heart continued to hammer and she began to fear that she could be letting herself in for something more than she could handle.

Zarek had a way of persuading her to do things against her will. Which meant that their marriage… She dared not let her thoughts go any further. She needed to remain cool and calm. She was the one doing the favour. She had the upper hand. Hadn't she just made everything clear?

The trouble was, Zarek was used to being in control. He could manage any situation—including a marriage of convenience! Her life as she knew it was unravelling. Two weeks ago she'd been happy and carefree. Two weeks ago she'd had a marriage to look forward to. Now she was still getting married—but to a different man! And for a very different reason.

It was the stuff of novels. Such things didn't happen in real life, not to someone like her. She looked at Zarek and then wished she hadn't when she saw the expression on his face. It was not the answer to her question that she wanted. 'I need to be alone,' she said.

'You have much to think about,' he agreed. 'But, Rhianne—' his eyes narrowed warningly '—don't think about changing your mind.'

She lifted her chin. 'I've given my word. You needn't fear that I'll go back on it.'

'Then I'll see you at dinner.' His voice followed her as she walked away. 'We can thrash out the wedding details then.'

The wedding was going to be one big rush, thought Rhianne as she threw herself down on the bed. A Greek wedding! She'd never attended one but she knew what they were like. Unless of course he was talking about some simple civil ceremony.

Actually, she couldn't see his parents settling for that. It would be an all-or-nothing affair.

Rhianne lay on the bed for a long time, staring at the whitewashed ceiling. The room was cool and a merciful relief from the heat outside, but her body was sizzling. Her emotions chaotic. What she ought to do was get up and run, and not stop running until she had reached some safe place in the world where she could relax and be herself. Where she could start a new life, alone and independent.

Except that she had given her word. She could not let Zarek down. She would honour him in front of his parents; they would never know that it was a loveless marriage.

But behind closed doors…

Rhianne did not let her thoughts go any further because she knew how persuasive Zarek could be. How he could set her pulses on a race through her veins, how he could make her heart feel as though it wanted to leap out of her chest, how he could send an impossible heat through every inch of her body.

Such disturbing thoughts had her leaping off the bed and straight under the shower. But even cold water did not calm her nerves. She was shivering by the time she had finished, but her mind was on a completely different tack.

A marriage ceremony!

A wedding night!

A honeymoon!

Would he expect this? She knew the answer. He would want his parents to believe that they were deeply in love, and he would do everything that normal, very-much-in-love couples did. And she would be expected to go along with it, to act like she had never acted before.

The more she thought about it, the more nervous she became, the more she wished that she had never come out here in the first place.

By the time Zarek came in search of her, she had slipped into a red silk strapless dress that should have clashed with her auburn hair but for some reason didn't. It was a dress she always felt good in, and she most definitely needed the armour now. 'I was just about to come down,' she said, unaware there was defensiveness in her tone.

'You look beautiful. Stunning, in fact.' His voice was a deep growl somewhere low in his throat. 'It will be an honour to marry you, Rhianne Pickering.'

'You're not forgetting that this won't be a real marriage?' Alarm filled her and, in contrast, Rhianne's voice rose sharply. She was right to be worried. He made it sound as though there was no way in the world he was going to honour her request.

'Of course not,' he answered swiftly.

'It doesn't sound like it.'

'I appreciate what you're doing more than you'll ever know.'

Rhianne wasn't so sure. The gleam in his eyes told her that he wanted her in his bed—and one way or another he intended doing precisely that. And unhappily she couldn't help wondering whether this whole marriage thing had just been an excuse.

Except that something told her she was being silly. She had never seen Zarek more sincere than when he had told her that there was a strong possibility the business could fall into his brother's hands. And after she'd met Christos she knew exactly why he was worried. The two men couldn't have been more opposite if they'd tried.

Over dinner, when she had expected him to talk more about his business fears, he spoke about their wedding instead. 'My mother will expect a full traditional wedding. A big family affair—uncles and aunts and cousins. Every relative you can imagine will be invited. Christos denied her that pleasure. He married Eugenia on the spur of the moment. I can't let my parents down.'

So the onus really was being put on her!

The future of Diakos Holdings was in her hands; that was what he was saying. And, on top of that, the wedding was going to be one very big sham. It didn't bear thinking about.

'Tomorrow you must get in touch with your parents and other family members. They must all come.'

'Are you telling me that you've already set a date for our marriage?' Her heart hammered in her breast, trying its hardest to escape. She felt as though she could hardly breathe.

'It will of necessity be very soon,' he told her. 'Probably within the next two weeks.'

Rhianne's eyes widened. 'And you think everyone can take time off at such short notice? If you must do things in such a hurry then I suggest a quickie wedding of some sort with just your parents present.' What was the point of such an extravaganza?

'So you don't intend telling your own parents? Is that what you're saying?' Harsh criticism entered his voice now, and his eyes lost their soft persuasiveness, became as hard as diamonds instead.

Rhianne shrugged. 'My mother lives in Seattle with her third husband. She's no recipe for a happy marriage. Why should I ask her? Why should she come all this way when it's a loveless marriage anyway? And my father, well, I have no idea where he is. He's a musician in a band and he travels the country.'

The harshness went, to be replaced by disbelief. 'That is the saddest thing I've ever heard. So in effect you're alone in the world?' He looked as though he wanted to take her into his arms, but he thought better of it, smiling faintly instead. 'More reason to make the most of our wedding. I'd like your parents to be present, but I can understand you not wanting to invite them.'

'I hadn't even got round to telling them I was marrying Angus,' she told him ruefully. 'I guess I would have done nearer the time but…'

'I can see how awkward it is for you,' he said. 'And I'm wondering how to tell my own mother about your predicament. Their marriage has been as strong as a rock. She truly believes in the sanctity of it, she would never have done anything to hurt my father.'

'Tell her the truth,' said Rhianne. 'I've never hidden the fact that my father cheated on my mother. So did her second husband. This last marriage has surprised me by its longevity. Though, actually, who knows what's happening. It could be on the rocks already. It's why I've always sworn that I'd only marry once I was very, very sure what I was doing.'

'And Angus let you down,' he said quietly.

Rhianne nodded, painful memories pushing to the surface.

'I would never do that.'

'It's hard,' said Rhianne, ignoring the way he was looking at her, 'finding your true soul mate. There's a whole world of men out there. How do you know which one you can trust?'

'I guess it's gut instinct,' said Zarek quietly, his dark eyes reaching out to hers.

Not wanting to read anything into them, Rhianne deliberately turned away. All this talk of weddings and families was getting to her. It seemed that the longer they talked, the deeper the hole she was digging for herself.

'My mother will smother you with love if I do tell her your story—which might not be a bad thing,' he added with a wry twist to his lips. 'Your life hasn't been happy. I'd suggest doing the loving myself but—'

He laughed when he saw indignation flare in her eyes. 'But I know my place. Not that I promise not to kiss you on our wedding day. We need to keep up appearances.'

It was a warning, thought Rhianne. She must be on her guard. Zarek was not a man to be easily ignored. If she wasn't careful, she would find herself swept off her feet, entering into the spirit of their marriage as though it was the real thing.

Dinner was a silent affair after that, each deep in their

own thoughts, Rhianne drinking far more Riesling than she was accustomed to. Zarek finally refused to pour her any more. 'Drowning your sorrows is not the answer.'

'Is that what you think I'm doing?' asked Rhianne, trying to look offended but fearing that she failed. She did feel inebriated, not that she wanted to admit it, but at least it allowed her to forget that she'd just agreed to marry a man she did not love.

'I think it's time you went to bed,' said Zarek.

Rhianne nodded. 'Good idea.' And she stood up, sitting again quickly when she discovered that her legs felt as though they were made of rubber.

Zarek's face didn't change. He simply got to his feet and offered his arm. 'May I escort my future wife to her room?'

Fearing he was mocking her, Rhianne glared into his eyes. She saw nothing but politeness. And she knew why he was pretending not to notice that she was drunk—because he didn't want to offend her! From now until the minute he married her he would bend over backwards to be nice.

What would happen after that was anyone's guess. She would be safe, though, tonight. He would take her up to her room and then leave her. He wouldn't dare try to take advantage. Even if he wanted to!

And Rhianne knew that he did. The kiss earlier had told her that he was hot for her. As she had been for him! Amazingly so! But hot sex did not constitute a good reason for marriage. And if she relaxed her code of ethics then she would never forgive herself.

They climbed the stairs together, his arm about her waist, and Rhianne held on to her thoughts with every shred of dignity that she could dredge up. It was hard when their bodies touched, when the heat of him filtered into her, making her hot too, when some little demon inside her head announced that she would be foolish not to let him kiss her again.

But she knew where a kiss could lead. Zarek had a way of making her forget her own set of rules.

It was with strength born of desperation that she said a firm, 'Goodnight,' and closed the bedroom door in his face.

But even though he wasn't with her in person, he remained with her in spirit. When she shrugged off her clothes and lay down on the big comfortable bed she couldn't stop herself thinking about him. And the fact that she'd agreed to marry him!

It was going to be the hardest thing she'd ever done. Zarek wasn't a man to live with a woman and not bed her. Even though he had promised, she was still fearful that he might not keep his word. Or that she might not want him to keep it!

She lay awake for a long time, listening to the faint call of a night bird, watching an almost full moon creep slowly across an inky sky, but then tiredness claimed her and her eyelids closed and soon she knew no more.

When morning came, she wondered whether all that had happened yesterday had been a dream. Surely she hadn't promised to marry Zarek? A man she hardly knew and certainly didn't love. It didn't make sense. She would never do such a thing; she was too sensible and level-headed.

At least, that was what she'd always thought.

But as soon as she saw him at the breakfast table, Rhianne knew that she was in dire trouble. Feelings came running back fast and furious. Feelings she had tried desperately to deny, to tell herself she didn't want.

He was dressed in a white T-shirt and a pair of denim jeans, which moulded to the shape of his body like a second skin. He was a lean, lithe man, with tight, hard muscles and not an ounce of superfluous fat. His London hotel had its own private gym, so she guessed that he must have used it on a daily basis to look so good. He'd possibly worked out all of his working life, and she remembered what it had felt like yesterday to be held against that hard muscular chest.

Her breath caught in her throat at the memory, and she had to forcibly tell herself that she must not let it happen again—or their convenient marriage would turn into a proper one. And that was the last thing she wanted because how could she possibly extricate herself from it if she had given herself totally to Zarek Diakos?

'Rhianne, good morning. You slept well, I hope? You certainly look refreshed.'

So did he! But she didn't tell him so. She was too busy fighting the demons within. Every time she looked at Zarek she was reminded that any day soon she would become his wife. The thought filled her with both fear and excitement.

'I slept very well, thank you.'

'That is good; I need you to be at your best this morning. We're going to see my mother and tell her about our wedding plans.'

CHAPTER EIGHT

'RHIANNE, Zarek, this is the best news I could ever have hoped for.'

Zarek's mother opened her arms wide and enveloped Rhianne, hugging her so tightly that she had to fight for breath.

'I knew you two were made for each other the moment I set eyes on you. This is a dream come true; you've made me so happy. We must go to the hospital straight away and tell Georgios. He'll be as excited as I am.'

Finally, she let Rhianne go and folded her son into her arms instead. 'Zarek, my darling son—I've waited so long for this day. Oh, I can't wait to start making arrangements. It's—'

'Mother,' protested Zarek, gently extricating himself, 'it's early days yet. I've only just proposed to Rhianne; please—'

But his mother was having none of it. She continued to talk excitedly, and Zarek looked at Rhianne and raised an eyebrow.

Rhianne had been nervous to begin with and she was even more so now. Even though Zarek had warned her about his mother, she hadn't been prepared for her over-the-top enthusiasm.

'Oh, my goodness,' the older woman kept saying, 'this is the best day of my life.'

The whole day was one big round of congratulations. Zarek's father was quietly happy for them, but his mother phoned every one of her family and told them the good news. And each time Zarek suggested they leave she persuaded him to stay a while longer.

'You cannot leave your poor mother now,' she kept saying. 'Not when you have just made me the happiest woman alive.'

Eventually, though, they managed to get away. 'My mother excelled herself,' declared Zarek, rolling his eyes as he glanced across at Rhianne. 'May I say how well you handled everything. I fully expected you to tell her it was all a sham and then run as fast as you could. And in truth, I wouldn't have blamed you. You were magnificent.'

Rhianne was glad that he was driving because she had the feeling that he wanted to thank her with kisses. The whole affair was escalating at an alarming rate, and she wasn't sure that she could handle it. She needed some time alone.

But Zarek had other ideas. As soon as they reached the villa he insisted she join him on the terrace where he opened a bottle of champagne. 'To my beautiful wife to be,' he said, raising his glass.

There was just the right amount of irony in his voice to remind Rhianne that it was all a game and yet, when he looked at her, his amazing dark eyes registered something more. And that something scared her. They had made a pact. Their marriage was to be in name only.

Nevertheless, she sensed a burning passion inside him and knew that she was in danger, not only from Zarek, but from a similar fever within herself. It was creeping up on her whether she liked it or not.

'I'm not sure I can go through with this.' She spoke the words without thinking, intending to say them to herself and not Zarek, and was startled when he slammed his glass down on the table with so much force that it was a wonder it didn't shatter into a thousand tiny pieces.

Rhianne watched as the champagne spilled over, fizzing onto the table top, each tiny drop spreading until they all merged into one. She knew that she dared not take her eyes from it; she did not want to look at Zarek, see his anger; know that she was creating a storm which could have severe repercussions.

But somehow he pulled himself together, and his voice was calm when he spoke to her. 'Every bride has nerves when she's about to get married. Every bride worries and wonders. Believe me, Rhianne, you'll be the most beautiful bride in the world, and it will be an honour to marry you.'

She raised her head, thinking he was mocking her, but saw nothing but sincerity in his eyes.

'My mother's enthusiasm has alarmed you, hasn't it?'

Rhianne nodded.

'I apologise on her behalf. I fear, though, that you'll have to get used to her exuberance. It's not every day her favourite son gets married.'

'It scares me,' she admitted.

'Perhaps this will help.'

Before Rhianne could sense his intention, Zarek got up from the table and pulled her to her feet. The next moment his lips were on hers, and there was nothing gentle or persuasive about his kisses this time.

Rhianne struggled with her conscience but couldn't fight the sensations that ricocheted through her body. Against her will she felt herself relaxing, her lips parting of their own volition, a whole volley of feelings exploding. It was both hell and heaven at the same time. She didn't want the kiss to stop but she knew the danger of letting it continue.

It seemed like forever before he finally set her mouth free. 'Does that allay your fears?'

Allay her fears? It scared her to death. She had felt an unexpected lightning response. He had awoken something primitive inside her that no other man had touched. In some strange way he had made her his.

'Rhianne?'

Realising that she hadn't answered him, Rhianne gave her head a tiny shake, struggling now to free herself. Not that it did her any good. Zarek's arms were like bands of steel, and she knew that he wouldn't let her go until she'd given him the answer he wanted.

'I'm all right,' she whispered, but she hated the fact that she had let herself be consoled by a kiss. The whole event was going to be one big roller-coaster ride of terror. She ought to have escaped while she had the chance.

There was no chance now. He had bound her to him with a kiss that had stirred senses she didn't know she possessed. They must have lain there dormant for years waiting for the right man to come along and discover them. She curled her fingers into her palms as she tried to make sense of the situation.

The right man wasn't Zarek; she wasn't ready for any

man. She didn't trust men. He was an expert seducer, that was all. He knew exactly what to do to get her onside. And, silly fool that she was, she had fallen for it.

She was committed now to the biggest marriage of the century, and she had to go through it with her head held high and a smile on her face.

'Good,' he growled. 'You're talking sense at last.'

And before she could stop him he kissed her again. Another mind-blowing kiss that had her straining against him, that sent her whole body into spasm, and there was a pleased smile on his face when he finally let her go.

For the rest of the day Zarek talked wedding plans, insisting that she contact her mother even though Rhianne swore she would not come. She was wrong. When her mother answered the telephone and heard the news she screamed her excitement.

'I thought you and Angus would never set the day.'

'It's not Angus, Mother. He and I are finished.'

There was a long silence while her mother assimilated this piece of information. Then she said more quietly, 'So who is he?'

'His name's Zarek Diakos and I'm here on the island of Santorini with him. We're having a Greek wedding, Mother. Next week, as a matter of fact. I hope you can come.'

Another scream from her mother. 'Next week? What's the rush? Are you pregnant?'

Rhianne almost laughed. 'Certainly not. But Zarek's father's ill, and if we wait too long he might not—'

Zarek gently took the telephone from her. 'Allow me.' And by the time he had finished talking to her, Rhianne's mother was won over.

'Of course I will come,' she said to Rhianne when Zarek

handed the phone back to her. 'My only daughter getting married, how could I not? Have you asked your father?'

'How can I when I don't know where he lives?' asked Rhianne sharply. 'I've not had a birthday or Christmas card from him in all the years he's been gone. It's his loss, not mine.'

Rhianne was glad when it was time for bed. So much had happened today that her head was spinning, and she longed for the solitude of her room. She needed to be alone with her thoughts.

Even then, when she found relative seclusion, she didn't feel any easier. It was hard to believe that she had allowed herself to be talked into marriage and on top of that Zarek had managed to awaken something inside her body that she had never discovered before.

It was the most frightening thing that had ever happened, and she even found herself wondering what it would be like to have Zarek make love to her.

Sleep was a long time in coming, and when she finally dropped off it was to dream about her forthcoming marriage. She dreamt that she wore the most outrageous wedding dress, Zarek only a pair of swimming briefs, and all the other guests were in fancy dress. It was bizarre and worrying, and when they went away on their honeymoon the whole family came with them.

She woke in a sweat and took a long, cooling shower. But she felt no better when, over breakfast the following morning, Zarek said that he was taking her shopping. 'You need to choose your wedding dress, otherwise my mother will insist on accompanying you. Her choice won't be yours, and I'm afraid she might force her decision on you.'

'I wouldn't let her,' declared Rhianne. 'But neither will I let you take me. It's bad luck for the groom to see his bride in her wedding dress before the day.'

'So who would you like with you?' He folded his arms across his broad chest and looked at her with a hint of amusement in his eyes. 'There is no one, is there?'

'I can wait until my mother gets here.'

Zarek shook his head. 'Too risky.'

'Then your driver can take me.'

Several long seconds passed. Their eyes met, and Rhianne felt a reincarnation of the desire she'd experienced last night. An aching need burned through her as she remembered his kiss, a kiss that had awoken new senses and told her how dangerous it was to tangle with this man.

She was right to insist that she shopped alone. Imagine what it would be like to parade before him in breathtaking wedding dresses. It wasn't the protocol thing she was worried about, it was Zarek's eyes feasting on her, taking in every curve of her body. Her insides tightened as she pictured the moment. Zarek sitting in a chair, his long legs stretched out in front of him, his eyes hooded as he scrutinized every tiny detail of each dress—and her body beneath it. Simply thinking about it whipped her emotions into overdrive.

'I'll meet you half way,' Zarek said finally. 'I'll drive you but I won't come into the shop. And after you've finished we'll find somewhere for lunch.'

'And would you really be content sitting outside while I pretend to be a happy bride to be?' She couldn't see it happening; she could imagine him sneaking into the shop and taking a crafty look.

His lips thinned dangerously. 'I don't want you to

pretend, Rhianne. I know it's unconventional but I want you to feel good about it too. You're at a hiatus in your life, why not treat this as a big adventure? You're in a win-win situation.'

He was right, though she was damned if she would admit it. They were playing games here, an exciting game, and she ought to grab it with both hands and make the most of it.

'Lunch it is then,' she agreed, and then almost wished she hadn't when she saw the gleam in Zarek's eyes.

Rhianne chose the plainest wedding dress she could find, unaware that its very simplicity was a stunning combination with her slender figure and glossy auburn hair. She had fixed it on top of her head this morning, but by the time she had tried on several dresses, long strands had escaped and curled flatteringly either side of her face.

Her colour was heightened too, and the service she received couldn't be faulted.

With one final look in the mirror before she took the dress off, Rhianne almost couldn't recognise herself. She was radiant, like a real bride. And she'd only had to mention Zarek's name and the sales women had fallen over themselves to be helpful.

Rhianne almost wished that she had let him come in with her. It didn't feel right to be trying on wedding dresses alone. She ought to have had a friend with her at least, but they were home in England and everything was so rushed.

True to his word, Zarek was waiting for her. 'All done?'

Rhianne nodded.

'You've chosen wisely?'

'Of course. And I've arranged to have the dress delivered. I didn't want it getting creased in the car while we have lunch. And thank you, Zarek, I didn't expect you to pay for it.' She hadn't been entirely surprised when she was told that he was settling the bill, and she'd had half a mind to insist that she pay herself. Until she saw how much the dress cost and realised it would practically empty her bank account.

'It is my pleasure,' he said, dark eyes hot and smouldering.

Rhianne fastened her seat belt and tried not to look at him. The whole experience had heightened her senses and she was more aware of him now than ever before.

The restaurant he took her to was hidden in a back street. They were early and had the room to themselves, and the proprietor looked after them personally. Rhianne hadn't felt hungry and she'd let Zarek order for her, but once the *kleftiko* lamb was placed in front of her, the fine smell alone had her taste buds salivating.

'Tell me about you as a little girl,' Zarek said, pausing between mouthfuls. 'Have you always had long hair, for instance? It's amazingly beautiful, do you realise that? My fingers are always itching to touch it.'

Heat invaded Rhianne's cheeks. It was not so much what he said but the way his eyes almost caressed her. She might even say they were making love, and it sent goose bumps across her skin and her senses skittering. 'For as long as I can remember,' she answered quietly and was horrified to hear a tell-tale tremble in her voice. 'Before my father deserted us I used to sit between his legs and he'd brush it and brush it until it shone.'

'How old were you when he left?'

'Ten, I think. Yes, I'd just had my tenth birthday. He wasn't there for it. I sensed there was something wrong, but didn't know until I was much older that he was having an affair.'

'It must have hurt you?'

Rhianne nodded. 'I adored him. I couldn't understand why he went away. For a long time I thought it was my fault.'

'And so you remained an only child?'

'Yes,' she answered sadly. 'My mother eventually married again, but they didn't have any children. Which is as well because he cheated on her the same as my father had, and she threw him out.'

'It would appear she doesn't have a very good taste in men. Either that or she's been extremely unlucky. How about husband number three?'

Rhianne wondered why he was asking all these questions. On the other hand, his relatives would be asking him about her at the wedding, and he'd need to be prepared. They hadn't even told his mother that they hardly knew each other.

'They're still married and, as far as I know very happy.'

'Do you have aunts and uncles? People we should invite to the wedding?'

'Both of my parents were only children,' she told him with a rueful smile. 'And to save you asking, no, I don't have any friends I want to invite either. I do have friends, naturally, but I have no wish to put myself up for all sorts of awkward questions.'

'You're ashamed of me?' A frown flitted across Zarek's forehead, pulling his dark brows into a formidable straight line.

'That would be impossible,' she answered with a tiny nervous laugh. 'You're any woman's dream.'

'Except yours?' he asked, the frown fading to be replaced by a wry smile.

Rhianne shrugged. 'I'm not ready for a serious relationship. I doubt I ever will be. And you can surely see why?'

Zarek nodded. 'I can, but not all men are the same. You and your mother have both had incredibly bad luck. But bad luck does not last. I would never hurt you, Rhianne. Whatever happens in our relationship, I promise you that.'

His eyes darkened with an emotion Rhianne could not read, and she felt a quiver sweep through her. When Zarek reached out across the table and took both her hands into his, the quiver deepened and became a rush of sensation. It careered through her veins setting off electric sparks at every vital point.

Unable to draw her eyes away from his, Rhianne allowed the feelings to run out of control, and it was not until she discovered that her lips were parted and were being moistened by the tip of her tongue, that her breathing had deepened and Zarek's eyes had dropped to the swell of her breasts, that she realised what was happening and immediately brought herself back to the present.

'I'm sorry,' she said, snatching her hands away from his.

'For what?' he asked softly. 'For allowing yourself a little pleasure?'

'I was not—I didn't—'

'Do not lie to me, Rhianne *mou*.'

'You're mistaken.'

'I think not. I think, Rhianne, that you're in denial. You do not think it right that you should feel something for me so soon after your tragic affair. But let me tell you something. The fact that you do feel—what shall I say—

an awareness, means that you never truly loved the man you were going to marry. You had a lucky escape.'

'And you're an expert in that sort of thing?' By this time Rhianne had come to her senses and sought anger to hide her embarrassment.

'I know a bit about women.'

'Not this woman.' Rhianne lifted her chin and fixed stony eyes on him.

A smile lifted the corners of his mouth. 'Then it will be my pleasure to find out.'

They were silent after that, and it annoyed Rhianne that Zarek's smile still lingered. She was glad when their dessert arrived: a sensational nut pie with a chocolate and orange sauce.

'That was truly delicious,' she acknowledged after she had eaten every last crumb, and when she looked around her she was startled to see that all the tables were now occupied. Zarek had been the sole focus of her attention, he had filled her every thought, her every breath, actually. Even here in this room, with the aroma of food wafting in from the kitchen, she was aware of Zarek's individual smell: clean and fresh and faintly musky. And she felt deeply shocked that he had managed to get through to her in this way.

Zarek ordered coffee and while they were waiting his cell phone rang. 'I'm sorry, do you mind?' he asked.

Rhianne shook her head, watching Zarek's face, realising that she was beginning to learn by his various expressions what sort of a mood he was in. When he was in a playful mood his eyes lightened to almost gold, his mouth softening; when he was serious his eyes narrowed and his mouth straightened. When he was angry his nostrils flared and his eyes became almost black. When he wanted to kiss her—Rhianne stopped herself there, not wanting to let her thoughts go down that channel.

Even as she watched him now she saw an entirely different expression. First the widening of his eyes then an instant narrowing as his brows drew together. His mouth grew tight and grim. 'I'll be right there,' he announced before shutting off his phone.

'We have to go.' He was already on his feet. 'My father's had another heart attack. It's touch-and-go whether he lives.'

CHAPTER NINE

Zarek feared for his father's health. He had looked so pale and lifeless yesterday that he had expected the worst.

His mother too was desperately worried and had clung to Zarek. Her son was her lifeline and she had asked him to stay with her. He had phoned Rhianne, not even thinking to ask whether she wanted to join them, simply telling her that he wouldn't be home.

But now he was on his way back to her, his father having improved during the night. He was still far from well but his colour had returned and he had been reasonably cheerful during Zarek's visit.

Rhianne came to greet him as he entered the villa, real concern on her face, and Zarek's heart lifted. Rhianne had no idea how beautiful she was, what simply looking into her eyes did to a man, or how very glad he was that he had met her.

'How is your father?' she asked at once.

'Much better this morning, thank you.' But Zarek was conscious of having neglected her, and Rhianne's well-being was his concern now. 'Did you sleep well? You weren't afraid in this house on your own?' His cook and cleaner came in on a daily basis, but it hadn't occurred to him that she might be uneasy sleeping here alone.

'I was fine,' she said with a smile that made his heart leap. She looked genuinely pleased to see him, which must surely bode well for their future?

There was something deep down inside him that suggested he would not want to let her go when the time came. He wasn't sure that he wanted to ever let her go, and it scared the hell out of him. A lifetime's commitment to one woman was something he had never entertained. Not once. Business had always came first; it was his main priority. It was his life!

If he'd thought at all about marriage, it was how could anyone possibly know whether they'd met the right person? How would you know it would last for the rest of your life? How did you know you would never grow tired of them?

Marriage was a risky business. Admittedly, his own parents were still very much in love after almost forty years, but that wasn't the norm. Rhianne's parents were a case in point. He didn't know what the statistics were these days, but he guessed that more marriages failed than lasted. Certainly most of his friends were divorced.

'I was worried about you,' he said. 'What have you been doing?'

Rhianne shrugged. 'I explored the neighbourhood, I swam in your pool, I read a little. I picked some flowers for the house.'

Zarek realised that before Rhianne, his villa had been like a heart without a soul. Empty. Spiritless. Now it had suddenly become alive.

Nothing had changed except Rhianne's presence, but

what a difference she had made. It hadn't happened straight away, not until she had sensed he wasn't a threat and relaxed, and yesterday she had even seemed to enjoy his company.

And this didn't take into account the response she'd made to his kisses! Every time he thought about it he felt knots in his stomach. Whether she knew it or not Rhianne was a dream to kiss. Totally different to other women.

Rhianne was special. Most females gave themselves to him easily, some even tried to force themselves on him. But not Rhianne. She had held back until she felt ready to let him kiss her.

And who was he trying to kid? Rhianne was suffering a broken heart. How could he forget that? Kissing him meant nothing. Certainly she wasn't ready to enter into a serious relationship. He was lucky she'd agreed to marry him.

'Are you a keen swimmer?' he asked.

'I enjoy it,' she replied, 'but I haven't done any in ages. It's usually when I go on holiday.'

The thought of Rhianne in her swimsuit sent a series of vivid pictures through his mind. He dashed them away before they did things to him that should never be allowed.

Her hair swung in an attractive ribbon of waves as she shook her head. 'You look as though you need to rest,' she said softly. 'Have you been at the hospital all night?'

'Most of it; I managed an hour or two at my mother's. I couldn't leave her, she was in such a state. I'm sorry I had to neglect you.' He opened his arms, half expecting her to ignore the gesture, feeling a rush of adrenalin when she stepped into them.

Rhianne didn't know what had prompted her to move so close to Zarek. Perhaps because she'd felt lonely without him. She had lied when she'd said that she hadn't felt fearful last night. Every little sound had had her pricking her ears; she'd almost been afraid to go to sleep.

It wasn't like being at home in England where everything was familiar. Here there were different sounds and smells. At night came the occasional soft bray of a donkey, the call of an unfamiliar bird, the faint sound of voices. And far, far below was the whisper of the ocean, calling, calling.

If Zarek's hug was supposed to be comforting it turned into something more. It started in her toes, the warmth spreading higher and higher, triggering each sensitive spot on its way until the whole of her body was infused with sensation.

It was almost impossible to keep still. She had the strongest urge yet to press herself against him. His arousal was hard and alarmingly evident, and whether it was the discovery that he too felt an echoing need, or whether it was her own feelings that terrified her, Rhianne wasn't sure, but she placed her hands flat against his chest ready to push herself away.

Before she could do any more than think about it, Zarek's arms tightened and his mouth made a move on hers. 'Mmm, you taste good.' He slid his hands down to her bottom and urged her even closer towards him.

Rhianne's mouth fell open in a shocked, 'Oh!' as she felt the force of his desire against her. 'We shouldn't be doing this.'

'Give me a good reason why not and I'll stop.' A wicked smile accompanied his words.

Rhianne knew that she ought to say that he was breaking his promise. But how could she when every inch of her was on fire, when need was growing greater than common sense?

'See,' he claimed triumphantly. 'You're simply denying yourself pleasure. Nevertheless, it will wait.'

And to her disappointment he let her go. She was shocked by her feelings and couldn't help wondering whether she was in danger of actually falling for Zarek. Admittedly, she thought of Angus less and less often, but that didn't mean she was ready for another relationship.

Did it?

The thought that she could be trapped in a loveless marriage filled her with dread. It had been okay when she had no feelings for him, when it was a business transaction and nothing more, when she knew that she could walk away at the end of it all with her heart whole and a healthy bank balance into the bargain.

But something was happening to her, something totally unexpected, and—

'Come,' he said, cutting into her thoughts. 'I know a beautiful little cove where we can swim to our hearts content. Have you had breakfast?'

'Not yet.'

'Then we'll eat out as well.'

'Do you really think we ought to leave the villa?' she asked tentatively. 'What if your father takes another turn for the worse? How will anyone get in touch with you if we're out?' Even as she spoke Rhianne wondered whether she was using this as an excuse not to go swimming with Zarek.

Visions of his fabulous naked torso flashed in front of her eyes. He was perfectly tanned and toned. He was every woman's dream. Not an inch of anything superfluous. So amazingly gorgeous that even thinking about him sent a bevy of butterflies through her stomach. It was a hot day, but she felt even hotter and dashed away her disquieting thoughts before they became reflected in her eyes.

'I'm always contactable, Rhianne. It's part of the job.' One eyebrow lifted, and his mouth quirked. 'Does that satisfy you?'

'I guess so,' she said quietly.

'Good. Go and get ready and we'll be on our way.'

The cliffs were high, the walk down to the cove steeply zigzagged, and the thought of climbing back up afterwards made Rhianne wish that she had suggested the pool. Except that the sea hadn't seemed quite so intimate.

As they walked she was faintly fearful of what the outcome of the day would be. Zarek merely hummed to himself. He was undoubtedly happy with the situation, and, knowing how hard he worked normally, and how worried he must be about his father, she was glad to see him relaxing and letting his hair down.

Even if it was to her disadvantage!

She felt that she was getting into a situation too big to handle. That one day she would regret every second of it. The attraction she felt for him, the fact that she feared she might be falling in love with him, made her fearful of every moment that they spent together.

He shouldn't be so damn sexy. He wasn't safe to be around. He aroused feelings inside her that were alien, that made a mockery of her virginal vows.

By the time they reached the cove Rhianne's thoughts were in chaos, but it wasn't until she shrugged off the wrap she had tied over her swimsuit that she realised to her horror that the clasp on her halter neck had broken. Her breasts were swinging bare!

Did she make an issue of it, declare that she wasn't going to swim after all, or take off the rest of her swimsuit and dart into the water as quickly as possible, hoping against hope that Zarek would not notice?

She chose the latter option, not even glancing at Zarek, running as if her life depended on it until the azure water of the Aegean swallowed her up. She swam and swam, intent only on getting as far away as possible.

Although she was a strong swimmer Zarek's long arms and powerful strokes soon brought him to her side. 'I didn't realise we were in a race.'

He had been surprised when he saw Rhianne run into the water stark naked. More than surprised. Faintly shocked if the truth were known. But excited too. If it was good enough for her then…

'It's not a race,' she said. 'I happen to enjoy swimming. Anyway, I knew you'd catch me up.'

'I'm enjoying the skinny-dipping experience,' he said with a grin, treading water at her side.

Rhianne looked down at him and her face went a fiery red. The water was too clear for her to be mistaken.

Zarek laughed. 'Don't be embarrassed. It's the best feeling in the world. We should do it more often.'

'The fastener on my swimsuit broke,' she told him defensively, looking somewhere over his shoulder instead of into his face.

'I'm glad. Anything to free you of your inhibitions, Rhianne. Have you ever swam naked before?'

She shook her head. No one had ever seen her without her clothes on, only her parents when she was a child. She had always thought that it was a mystique to be shared in marriage. It was ironic under the circumstances.

For several long minutes they swam and played in the water, Zarek gently brushing his body against hers, nothing to alarm her; she couldn't even be sure that it was deliberate. She was actually enjoying herself, relaxing in a way she had never thought possible.

Zarek was making it easy for her. Even though she knew he must be worried about his father he was relaxed and fun, and when he finally suggested that they head back to shore she didn't want the pleasure to stop.

And, amazingly, when they reached the shoreline and strode up to where they had left their clothes, she still did not feel embarrassed. Something had happened out there, something that had brought them closer together. It was not a physical intimacy but a mental one; they had crossed a line, and, as she wrapped her caftan around her, and Zarek pulled on his shorts and T-shirt, she felt that it was almost a shame that they must dress.

She had become a free spirit out there in the clear waters, she had let the love she was beginning to feel for this man shed her inhibitions, but now, with her body covered, Zarek's too, it was almost like a step back. This was the man she was marrying purely to protect his inheritance.

Reality set in once again.

The dark cliffs that enclosed the beach seemed to have moved in on them, making Rhianne feel trapped. There was not another soul about, and she knew they had a long climb back up. The turquoise sea, which had been so inviting earlier, was now her enemy. Trapping her in this tiny space with the one man who had managed to turn her blood to water so that it raced through her body at lightning speed.

'Let's go,' he said softly, almost as though he had read

her thoughts, was aware of her sudden fear, and he began to lead the way back up the hillside.

Their strenuous climb took them to a tiny café where he was on good terms with the owner.

'And this is your—er—girlfriend?' the man questioned Zarek.

'My future wife,' he claimed proudly. 'Rhianne, this is Nikos, we grew up together.'

'Congratulations,' said Nikos. 'This is a good man; you have made a wise choice.'

As soon as he had gone Rhianne glared. 'I wish you hadn't told him we were getting married. It's not as if it's for real.'

'No one knows that,' he answered solemnly, reaching out for her hands and touching his lips to the back of them.

Light though the kisses were, they sent electrical impulses sizzling through her veins, making her clamp her thighs and buttocks tightly together, terribly conscious that she wore nothing beneath her caftan. She was growing more aware of him with each hour that passed, and it troubled her deeply.

'We need to keep up the pretence of our relationship being the real thing,' he explained, 'because once word gets around that we're married everyone will want to know who you are. Why not tell them now?'

'It just doesn't feel right,' she said quietly, sadly.

'I thought we'd reached a turning point out there.'

Rhianne felt her cheeks grow warm as his eyes rested questioningly on her face, but she didn't answer his question. How could she admit that she too had felt—something? A whole lot of something! Something that scared her half to death.

A few moments later their breakfast arrived. Greek yoghurt beaten with honey, fresh figs with goat's cheese and bread still warm from the oven. It was a simple breakfast but one of the nicest Rhianne had ever eaten.

'That was truly delicious,' she said, sitting back.

'Simple is often the best.'

'So why can't we have a simple wedding instead of the massive extravaganza you're planning?' she retorted.

'You think my mother would allow it?'

Rhianne giggled; she couldn't help herself. Here was a man right at the top of his profession, in control of goodness knows how many companies, and he was worried about what his mother might think.

'Why are you laughing?'

'Because I can't imagine you being frightened of your mother.'

'If you knew her as well as I do then you'd be frightened too,' he said, his brows rising comically. 'When Christos and I were little we were frequently in trouble. My father rarely scolded us; it was always my mother.'

'At least you had both your parents.'

'That's true. It must have been hard for you when your father left.'

'It was at first,' she admitted, 'but I got tough. I had to. I became my mother's little helper.'

'I'm looking forward to meeting her. Do you look like your mother?'

Rhianne laughed. 'Not at all. I have some of my father's features. I have his eyes and forehead.'

'And your hair?' His voice, which had gone deeper as he spoke, tailed off as he reached out and knotted a lock through his fingers each side of her face.

His eyes held hers.

Rhianne stopped breathing.

Then he pulled gently until her face was very close to his, until she could see every pore, smell the freshness of him, feel his heat. See the gold flecks in his eyes. He was going to kiss her, without a doubt he was going to kiss her, and considering how high her emotions were running she wouldn't be able to stop him.

The situation was getting out of control. He was playing unfairly.

'Don't do this, Zarek,' she said quietly.

'Nikos is watching us,' he returned equally as quietly. 'We need to act as though we're very much in love.'

She didn't believe him for one second. He was doing this because he wanted to. And, heaven help her, she wanted it too.

Why she felt like this when only two weeks ago her life had been destroyed, when she had felt she would never trust a man in her whole life again, she didn't know. She was getting carried away by this beautiful place and Zarek's persistent attention. He was such a charmer that no woman in her right mind could possibly resist him.

But it was all a game as far as he was concerned. He'd just admitted that he needed to keep up appearances. She wished he would stop to think what it was doing to her. He was exciting sexual emotions that she didn't want, had never felt before, at least not to this extent. No one had ever set her body on fire like this, not with just a look. Zarek's eyes were seriously disturbing, sending out silent signals that triggered a deep and unexpected response. Heaven help her when they were married if he carried on like this.

'I don't care who's watching,' she said, still speaking

quietly. 'I don't feel comfortable.' And if he didn't stop right now she would get up and leave. Let Nikos think what he liked.

For a long moment he didn't speak. He simply continued to look deeply into her eyes. Then with a mysterious little smile he relaxed his fingers. Her hair swung back and brushed her cheeks. A feather-light touch, almost as though it was Zarek's hand caressing her.

Rhianne swallowed hard and sat back, closing her eyes momentarily, trying to bring her emotions under control.

'It's time we went.' Zarek's voice ruptured the silence. 'I'll take you to my mother's; you can help her with the wedding preparations.'

It was a good idea; Rhianne knew she ought to be doing something. In fact, she ought to be the one doing everything. The trouble was she feared that his mother would ask so many personal questions that she wouldn't be able to carry on lying.

'Won't she be at the hospital?' she asked, mentally crossing her fingers.

'We'll check there first,' he answered. 'And, Rhianne,' he warned, 'don't let me down.'

CHAPTER TEN

THE next few days passed quickly. Rhianne duly helped Zarek's mother with the arrangements, and even though she was ridiculously nervous in case she gave the game away she managed to give a creditable performance of being the happy bride to be.

Georgios's health improved as well, and it looked likely that he would be able to attend the wedding.

Zarek remained the pure gentleman. Polite and kind but nothing more. Which should have pleased her but instead dismayed her, and she couldn't help wondering whether it was because she had said that she didn't like him touching her in public. She had meant it at the time—she'd felt embarrassed by his attention—but now she began to wish that she had never spoken.

On the day before the wedding, her own mother arrived. 'Darling,' her parent enthused, 'you're looking wonderful, positively radiant, in fact.'

Rhianne didn't feel radiant, she felt distinctly uneasy. Conversely, her mother was more elegant than she had ever seen her, in a smart Chanel suit with her auburn hair cut fashionably short.

'So this is where you're living?' she asked, looking around her with interest. 'Zarek must be extremely wealthy to own a place like this. Where is this magnificent man? I'm dying to meet him.'

'Mother, I hope you don't talk to Zarek like that. He—'

'Your mother, dearest Rhianne, can talk however she likes.'

Zarek walked into the room, having clearly heard and liked the 'magnificent' bit.

He kissed her mother's hand in a gallant gesture. 'Now I can see from where Rhianne gets her good looks. I trust you had a good flight? Your room is ready; I'll arrange to have your luggage sent up while you talk to your daughter. Drinks on the terrace, perhaps?'

Her mother was instantly won over. 'What a charming man,' she said to Rhianne once he had disappeared. 'Do tell me how you two met. And what happened to Angus? What did you fall out over?'

Rhianne gave a brief version of events, avoiding any questions she didn't want to answer, and was glad when Zarek rejoined them.

For the next hour he entertained her mother, and Rhianne was able to sit back and listen to their conversation. Then jet lag caught up and her parent announced that she would like to take a rest before dinner.

Rhianne was relieved. Her mother had watched the two of them keenly, and Rhianne had been forced to act as she had never acted before. She had flirted with Zarek, she had even sat on his lap at one stage and linked her arms around his neck.

In response he had tilted her chin and kissed her, an amazing kiss that had sent Rhianne's hormones running frantically. There was hard evidence that it had affected Zarek too!

'If I didn't know you better,' said Zarek once they were alone, 'I would think that you were beginning to feel something for me. That was quite a little performance you put on.'

Rhianne said nothing. It had been no act. She had only to look at him these days for her body to hunger for him. But she had no idea what Zarek's true feelings were. And now that the wedding was less than twenty-four hours away, she was scared to death that he would want her in his bed. And how could she deny him, feeling as she did?

'If you carry on like that tomorrow,' he said now, his voice low and husky, 'you'll make everything so much easier. Can you imagine what it would be like trying to convince everyone that we're deeply in love if we felt nothing for each other?'

'You're saying that you feel something for me?' Rhianne's heart began to race.

Zarek guarded his eyes. 'I'm saying, Rhianne, that we've made a connection. So much so that we'll be able to fool everyone that we're in love. I'm deeply grateful to you.'

Rhianne swallowed hard. Grateful! He had no idea what was really going on inside her head.

'And think what you'll be getting out of it,' he continued. 'A home here and in London. An allowance that will let you buy anything you want—a trip to America to see your mother, for instance. And by the way, is your father coming?'

His quick change of subject took Rhianne by surprise. 'Heavens, no!' Her whole face filled with scorn. 'He's ignored me all these years, so as far as I'm concerned he's no longer my father.'

Zarek groaned and gathered her against his hard chest. 'I'm sorry. I find it hard to believe that any man could abandon his family.'

'My mother's agreed to step into his shoes,' she told him as mixed signals shot through her brain.

It felt like a game she had played as a child when she was thinking about the best-looking boy in her class. One by one she had pulled the petals off a daisy and chanted, he loves me, he loves me not, he loves me, he loves me not.

She really did not know how to take Zarek. Was he simply using her or was he not? Was he beginning to feel something for her or was he not? Sometimes she thought he was, but at other times she was convinced that it was nothing but a game to him. A serious game because his future success depended on it, but a game all the same.

It, oddly, hurt to think this, especially as her feelings towards him were changing. As far as he was concerned he was buying a wife. And she must remember that. A wife in name only!

She was the one doing the favour, so she could call the shots.

Easier said than done. Especially when everything around her faded into insignificance, when she was aware only of Zarek's throbbing body next to hers. Was it his heart pounding or her own? Perhaps both in unison.

'I'm relying on you, Rhianne, to get through tomorrow without letting me down. The future of Diakos Holdings is in your hands.'

Why did he feel the need to keep reminding her? It

was the only reason she was still here. Except that when she had agreed to the contract she hadn't expected to experience these strong feelings. They terrified her.

'And by the way, I'm going to sleep at my parents' house tonight. Your mother reaffirmed that it was bad luck to see my bride before the ceremony.'

Rhianne's eyes opened wide. 'You cannot leave me, Zarek. How will I know where to go, what to do?' Now that the big moment was almost upon them a swift ribbon of fear flowed through her veins.

'I will never leave you, Rhianne.'

There was a deepness to his voice that she hadn't heard before. It came from low in his throat, and it sent a shiver over her skin.

Zarek came to his senses just in time. Holding Rhianne against him and feeling the exciting warmth of her body, inhaling the floral shampoo she'd used on her hair, was leading him into temptation. For just a moment he had been lulled into believing that their marriage was real. It was time to take a step back and reassess himself.

'I will never leave you in the lurch,' he amended, relaxing his arms and letting her back out of them. 'As far as the actual wedding is concerned, tomorrow my whole family, including the priest, will walk over here. Christos is best man, did I tell you that? He will then lead the party from here to the church.'

'Why Christos?' asked Rhianne fiercely. 'Don't you have a friend who could do it?'

'My parents would never forgive me. Don't worry, he'll behave himself. He wanted to know why I'd decided to get married so suddenly. I told him it was love at first sight and we saw no reason to wait. You're quite something,

Rhianne, do you know that? Not many people would give up their life to help someone they hardly know.'

His feelings for this beautiful woman were growing deeper by the day. He wasn't sure whether it was actually love he felt, or a very, very deep desire to possess her. She was certainly the only woman ever to make him feel like this.

'We're foregoing some of the traditions because of my father's health; it would be too much for him.'

'Thank you,' said Rhianne quietly, turning to look out of the window towards Oia, picking out the blue-domed roof of the church where she would soon become Zarek's wife. It was a daunting thought, and she was really glad that her mother was here. She felt so alone, so vulnerable. Zarek wasn't forcing her into this; she could have said no anywhere along the way. But even so…

They finished their drinks, and Rhianne stood up. 'I don't think I'll sleep tonight.'

'Me neither,' he said, unfolding himself too. 'It will be a big day. And, Rhianne, I really do appreciate what you're doing for me. I know it's a lot, and I know you'll be putting your life on hold, but words cannot express my gratitude.'

Rhianne wasn't sure whether he reached out to her or whether it was the other way round, but she found herself in his arms. His mesmerising eyes looked deep into hers, one hand rising to caress the side of her face, and Rhianne found herself pressing her cheek into his palm. It was pure instinct that drove her, especially when she lifted her own hand and placed it on top of his.

She expected a kiss to follow, wanted it even, but Zarek did no more than touch his lips to her brow. 'Goodnight, *agapi mou.*'

'Goodnight, Zarek.'

Neither of them moved.

Their eyes locked, and Rhianne felt as though all the breath was being sucked out of her body. Zarek was the first to break the invisible bond. He pressed a kiss to his first and second fingers and touched them to her lips. 'Go get your beauty sleep. I'll see you tomorrow.'

The morning of their wedding day dawned bright and clear. Rhianne was understandably nervous, her mother even more so. 'I feel that I should have done more towards this wedding of yours. Zarek's family will judge me.'

'How could you do anything from so far away?' questioned Rhianne. 'They understand. Zarek's father's been ill—it was touch and go whether he lived at one time—and Zarek wanted to ensure that he saw us happily married. In any case, Zarek's mother enjoyed making all the arrangements. I didn't do very much myself, to be honest.'

'You're lucky, my darling, to have found someone like Zarek.'

'And you, Mum, how is your marriage?' Rhianne didn't want to keep on talking about Zarek as though he was the love of her life.

Her mother's eyes shadowed. 'We're going through a tricky patch. David's been playing away. What is it with me and men, Rhianne?'

'Perhaps it's all men,' she said sadly.

'I'm sure Zarek won't let you down. I've seen the way he looks at you; he loves you dearly, and I know I'm not a very good judge of character where my own affairs are concerned, but I feel that his values are all in the right place. Have a happy day, my darling, and a lifetime of happiness to follow.'

Her mother wasn't usually this sentimental. For one tiny moment Rhianne thought about telling her the true story, but Zarek's face flashed in front of her eyes, and she knew that she couldn't do this to him. Instead, tears begin to well. 'Will you come and help me get ready?'

Zarek had sent in a hairdresser to fix her hair and a beautician to do her makeup and nails, but when a dresser turned up as well Rhianne politely but firmly sent her away. She wanted no one but her mother.

When they had finished, Rhianne hardly recognised herself. She looked more beautiful than ever in her life. Taller too in the body-skimming dress. Then her mother handed her a white satin box. 'Zarek asked me to give you this.'

When Rhianne opened it she gasped. A diamond necklace with matching drop earrings that must have cost the earth. He really had gone to town, while she had bought him nothing. It hadn't seemed appropriate under the circumstances. She had a wedding ring for him, but that was all, and they'd chosen that together when he had bought her ring.

Her mother too was open-mouthed in disbelief.

By the time the wedding procession arrived Rhianne was ready. Her eyes met Zarek's and everything inside her went on to high alert. He looked devastatingly handsome in an ivory dress suit, and she felt a momentary stab of pain that this wasn't going to be a permanent marriage.

Christos led the procession to the church; Rhianne followed behind with her mother escorting her. She presumed Zarek was close behind but she didn't look around. She couldn't. She felt stiff with fear now. This was a big thing she was doing and it was too late to back out. Then she heard his voice in her ear, felt his warm breath on the back of her neck. 'You're doing well, Rhianne. I'm proud of you.'

It was enough to make her stand that little bit straighter and hold her head high. She fixed a smile on her lips and walked into the church.

It was filled to overflowing, and Rhianne was glad when the long ceremony was over. She had felt her whole body tremble as she'd made her vows. It was the most difficult thing she'd ever had to do. Zarek, on the other hand, had acted as though he were really in love; it had shone from his eyes as he looked at her.

On the way to the hotel for the champagne reception he squeezed her hand. 'Thank you, Rhianne,' he said quietly. 'I don't think I've told you how stunning you look. Truly the radiant bride. I've had so many compliments on my choice of wife. You've done me proud.'

'It's all part of the service.' God, she hated herself for saying this, but she had to keep up the act or else she would begin to doubt whether this marriage was a fake one or for real. 'And thank you for the jewellery. It's dazzling, but I won't be able to keep it. I trust you had it on sale or return?'

She heard the whoosh as he took a sudden harsh intake of breath. 'Rhianne, they are yours. To keep or do with as you like.'

At the hotel she was overwhelmed by the welcome she was given by the various members of his family. The impression she got was that they had all thought Zarek would never get married. Some of them spoke a little English, most none at all, but they all shook her hand or gave her a hug and let her know that she was now one of them.

After their meal there was lots of traditional dancing that Rhianne had to fake her way through. Every man in the room claimed a dance with her, and when it was Christos's turn he wanted to know how they had met. 'My brother always said he was married to his work and would never take himself a wife. You must have something special.'

'I guess we have,' answered Rhianne with a sweet smile. 'Zarek is a very special man.'

'A very wealthy man as well.'

A frown quickly furrowed her brow, and her heart did a double beat. 'Are you suggesting that I'm marrying your brother for his money? You insult me. I—'

Before she could say any more Zarek took her elbow, his dark eyes narrowed and hard. 'Do not talk to my wife like that, brother, or you'll regret it. There is only one reason Rhianne and I have married and that's because we're both very much in love. Any more of that sort of talk and I won't be accountable for my actions.'

He dragged Rhianne away. 'I'm sorry about that. Christos was out of order. He's jealous, that's his trouble. You've met his wife, have you? She's a sourpuss. I think he's regretting marrying her. But I thank you for your support.' He pulled her into his arms and kissed her. Nothing deep, a thank you kiss, a mere touching of his lips to hers. But it awoke a treacherous desire, and she clung to him, her mouth softening and opening. She heard his faint groan, but before he could enter they were surrounded by laughing, clapping people.

'It's what they've been waiting for,' he said against her lips. 'They want to see a show of our love. We must not disappoint them.' Nor did he. His kiss was spectacularly passionate. Rhianne forgot for the moment that they were being watched and gave herself up to the mind-blowing pleasure he was giving her, linking her arms around his neck, gyrating her body against him, very much aware of an arousal that both thrilled and shocked her.

His tongue explored and teased in a kiss far deeper than any other he had given her—and all in front of an audience! Whether it was an act on Zarek's part, she wasn't sure, but, whatever, she was most definitely having trouble hiding the fact that her most basic instincts were surfacing.

When he finally set her free, when the floor show was over, a further bout of spontaneous clapping took place.

Then the money dance began. Zarek had warned her about this. Everyone pinned money to their clothes as they danced their way around the floor, and Rhianne thought the evening was never going to end.

But finally they managed to make their exit. A car was waiting to take them home, and it was then that Rhianne's real fears began.

Her heart beat loudly when Zarek led her straight upstairs. The door to his bedroom had been left tantalisingly open, and the first thing she saw was a diaphanous nightie laid out on his bed.

'What is this?' she asked, her throbbing heart feeling heavy in her chest.

'What does it look like?'

'But ours isn't a real—'

'Shh!' Zarek placed a gentle finger on her lips. 'Rhianne, *agapi mou*, you've shown me in a thousand different ways how you feel about me. Your lips might lie but your body doesn't. Do not be afraid.'

CHAPTER ELEVEN

Do not be afraid!

The words echoed inside Rhianne's head, going round and round until she felt dizzy. But it wasn't Zarek she was afraid of, it was her own feelings. Each day she had spent in this man's company they had spiralled and grown until she knew that she couldn't last much longer without letting him make love to her. Her moral innocence, that she had treasured so much, was a thing of the past. Zarek had whipped her body into a frenzy of need and desire from which there was no escape.

But even though she desperately wanted him to make love to her, she also knew in her own mind that if he did, there would be no going back. He would expect her in his bed every night.

For the duration of their marriage.

Big warning bells rang in her head. Not so much rang as clanged—loudly! She clapped her hands to her ears to stop the distressing sound.

'Rhianne, what's wrong?' Zarek took her face between his palms, deep concern in his eyes. 'Do you have a headache? The day has been too much for you. Come, come and sit down, I'll get you some aspirin and—'

'No, Zarek. I don't have a headache, I'm in a state of shock. Can't you see that?' She pulled away from him, burning from his touch but still feeling a need to protect herself. 'What's happened to your promises?'

'Naturally, they still hold,' he said with a faint quizzical frown. 'I won't do anything you don't want me to do.'

'But all this.' She indicated the bed, the rose petals scattered over the pillows, the chocolates, the bottle of champagne waiting on ice.

'It can go. I thought you might—'

'You thought wrong, Zarek,' she interrupted him sharply. 'You know how I feel. I don't want to sleep with you.' Even as she spoke Rhianne's body ached with a need that scared her to death.

Walking back to the door, he held it open. 'Feel free to go to your own room,' he said, his lips tightening, and something she didn't want to see locked into his eyes.

He knew, she thought, he knew she wouldn't go in there and sleep by herself. How could she after today? That kiss on the dance floor—it had knocked her sideways. She had given herself away. And he was aware of it. He was calling her bluff.

She heaved a sigh and sat down. 'I'd like some champagne. I was too afraid to drink much today in case I got drunk and made a fool of myself.'

Zarek looked at her, his expression softening. 'I don't imagine you've ever got drunk in your life, nor made a fool of yourself—except perhaps when you walked in front of my car. And that was my gain.'

Yes, it was his gain, and in some indefinable way it was also hers. She smiled weakly, watching as he opened the bottle and poured the sparkling liquid into elegant crystal flutes. But when he passed her drink and their fingers touched she no longer felt weakness. Fire ignited and raced out of control through her body.

'My sweet Rhianne,' said Zarek, briefly touching his hand to her face. 'Maybe it's time you got out of that dress and into something you can relax in. But before you do, in case I didn't tell you earlier, you look stunning. I didn't expect such a simple dress—I thought something frothy and extravagant—but it is perfection. No other words can describe it. You are beautiful.'

Rhianne caught a glimpse of herself in the mirror across the room. Her cheeks were flushed and her hair was awry, but her eyes were bright and, yes, she did look beautiful, more beautiful than she'd ever looked in her life. On the other hand, she'd never before worn a dress that had cost as much as this. It would make any woman look good. She almost didn't recognise herself.

She looked like a woman in love!

Her fingers reached up to touch the beautiful diamond necklace at her throat, and she wondered when she would wear such a striking piece of jewellery again. And the earrings, long droppers that sparkled magnificently in the light, what sort of an event would she need to attend to wear them?

She hadn't even realised that Zarek had moved to stand behind her until she saw his face reflected above hers. He laid his hands on her shoulders and more flames of fire licked their way through her entire sensory system, growing in intensity with each passing second.

Without even realising what she was doing Rhianne lifted her hands to touch his, causing a further whirlpool of rich emotion, and when she caught her reflection she was shocked to discover that her feelings were echoed clearly for Zarek to see.

Her eyes had gone from bright to overbright, the colour in her cheeks had heightened, and her lips were parted and moist. Strange, she couldn't remember passing her tongue across them, though she must have done. Her heart was pounding so erratically that she thought it might leap out of her chest.

Without a word Zarek hauled her into his arms, and when he kissed her Rhianne was surprised to feel how gentle his lips were. She had known this was going to happen and that she wouldn't be able to stop him, but she had expected blazing passion.

All day she had been aware of his hunger. It had flared in his eyes whenever he'd looked at her. And each time she had felt a dizzying response. It was not something that could be ignored, try as she might.

The tenderness of his kisses, however, made no difference to the sensations swirling in her head. She clung to him for support and realised that somewhere along the way he had discarded his jacket and bow tie, and that the first few buttons of his shirt were undone, revealing his dark chest hair.

She had the urge to touch, to find out what it was like to feel those whorls of springy hair beneath her fingertips. These were alien feelings and yet, conversely, they felt right. Everything felt right tonight.

It had been a day without parallel, a day she would remember for the rest of her life—regardless of what happened in the future.

Unconsciously she pressed her body closer to his, feeling some of his heat spread into her, feeling her bones begin to melt. And it alarmed her to discover that she wanted still more. More of this man, more of everything he had to offer.

She threaded her fingers into the thickness of his hair, pulling his head closer so that their kisses grew harder and wilder, their lips parting hungrily. His tongue tasted and sensitised the inside of her mouth, creating new pleasures, inviting more, expertly seducing her. Rhianne's fingers trailed down to his nape, feeling the faint rasp where he'd had his hair cut short for their wedding, and then on to his shoulders where muscles were bunched.

She didn't realise that Zarek had been gradually undoing the long line of buttons at the back of her dress until she felt his fingers on her naked skin. A ripple of sensation ran through her, and she wanted to be free of the dress's encumbrance, free to feel Zarek's hands on every part of her body. Her head fell back and her eyes closed, her lips were parted and moist, and she shrugged her shoulders to allow the dress to slip to the floor.

Zarek groaned. All day long he had waited for the moment when Rhianne became his. He'd not been sure that it would happen, but the kiss on the dance floor had given him hope. His hopes had been dashed when Rhianne declared she wanted separate rooms, and he'd almost thundered that he would allow no such thing. How he'd held back those words he did not know, but now he was glad that he had. Rhianne was responding to him of her own free will. There had been cracks in the composure she had tried her hardest to retain, but now they were wide open, and it looked as though tonight she would be sharing his bed after all.

He dared not let himself go down the road of what

would happen in the future. His main aim had been to safeguard the business, and he'd achieved that. Now his aim was to keep Rhianne happy—and, hopefully, in his bed. He couldn't possibly sustain the marriage if Rhianne didn't allow him to touch her—not when he was in grave danger of falling in love with her. A thought that filled him with both pleasure and fear at the same time!

As she stepped out of the dress he took her hand, feeling her tremble, seeing the uncertainty in her eyes. All she wore now was the briefest of white bras and a G-string, and sheer stockings that looked as though they were held up by willpower. Her body was long and slender and faintly tanned, and his whole being went onto high alert simply looking at her.

With a groan he pulled her against him, making her aware of the hard force of his erection. In response, a quiver ran through Rhianne's entire body, and a strangled sound escaped her throat as her head fell back. He pressed his lips to the tantalising arch, tasting the sweet fragrance of her skin, touching his tongue to the rapid beat of her pulse, and slowly but surely moving lower and lower, one hand against her back now, the other cupping one softly rounded breast.

When it became clear that Rhianne was not going to stop him, that she appeared to need this as much he did, he snapped the fastening on her strapless bra and watched in total fascination as it slowly dropped away to reveal breasts that were firm and beautifully formed, with tight dark pink nipples already on high alert.

He felt her sway backwards as he lowered his head to take one of her nipples into his mouth, delighting in the soft helpless little sounds she made deep in her throat.

'Not only do you look beautiful, *agapi mou*,' he groaned, 'you taste beautiful too.'

Rhianne was unaware of Zarek manoeuvring her across the room; she was conscious only of the flood of sensation streaking through her body like a jet across the sky. It was not until he sat down on the edge of the bed, urging her towards him so that her legs were wide as they straddled his knees, that she realised what he was doing.

From this vulnerable position he continued his assault on her breasts, and as he sucked each nipple in turn into his mouth, as he teased them with his tongue and teeth, Rhianne grew almost faint. This was an experience too far. Zarek was turning this marriage into a proper one.

He was claiming her as his bride in every way!

So why didn't she stop him?

The answer was simple. She couldn't. Zarek was an expert in the pleasure stakes. He must have known that once he began she wouldn't want him to stop. Her fingers threaded through his short springy hair, clutching the fine shape of his head. In contrast, her own head was thrust back, her eyes closed as she lapped up the attention he was paying her.

When his mouth moved lower, trailing hot kisses over her stomach, pausing for a moment while his tongue explored her belly button, where she discovered a high state of sensitivity that she had never known existed, she couldn't find the strength to stop him, and when she heard the snap of material as he tore off her G-string, she knew that she had gone too far now to back out.

Zarek was drawing her into his web like a spider did a fly. Irrevocably. She had become his to do with as he liked.

Somewhere, deep, deep down inside her, she still did have a mind of her own, but she didn't want to listen to it.

With one swift, deft movement Zarek reversed their positions. She was the one on the edge of the bed now and he was kneeling. Almost reverently his tongue touched and stroked the most intimate part of her, and the pleasure was so alien and so exquisite that she thought she was going to faint.

She lay back, reeling as wave after wave of electrifying sensations flooded the lower part of her stomach, reaching out long, intense fingers to excite other parts of her body.

Zarek lifted her legs over his shoulders and continued to taste and tease her with his hot, eager tongue, and Rhianne became lost in a world of feelings that made her feel as though her body no longer belonged to her.

It seemed an age before he finally stopped, a whole lifetime, and when he slowly drew her to her feet Rhianne was unable to stand. Every bone in her body had melted and she was compelled to cling to Zarek for support.

She wore nothing but her stockings and high heels, whereas he was still fully clothed. His face, though, mirrored her own. His lips were soft and moist, his eyes as black as night. 'I think,' he said gruffly, 'that that's enough for now.'

Rhianne couldn't believe the disappointment she felt. Instead of feeling relieved that he was going to take it no further, she contrarily wanted more. He had shown her pleasure on a scale she had never felt. He couldn't end it here, she wouldn't let him.

'Oh, no,' she said, looking him straight in the eye, 'it's not over yet.' With great daring she began to unbutton his shirt, and as each inch of flesh was exposed she layered kisses on to his burning skin, not stopping until she had his shirt fully open. With impatient fingers she tugged it out of his waistband and off his shoulders and threw it to the floor.

Then she began rubbing herself against him, her hips against the part of him that throbbed and pulsed and needed urgent attention, her aching breasts against his chest, enjoying the roughness of his body hair on her tender skin. She had never done anything like this before—it was as though Zarek had woken a siren inside her.

His groans were deep, his eyes dark and glazed. With unsteady hands he twisted a length of hair through his fingers, using it to pull her head close to his so that he could take and taste her lips in a hard kiss that ground her lips back against her teeth until she tasted blood.

Rhianne began to undo his belt buckle. Her fingers felt shaky and awkward, but somehow she managed it, then the clip on his trousers, followed swiftly by the zip. The sound it made was heightened by the atmosphere in the room. The air around them had thickened and was full of tension, but there was no stopping Rhianne now.

Zarek hopped obligingly out of his trousers, kicking off his shoes and socks as he did so. But it was left to Rhianne to take off his black briefs. She did wonder for a few seconds whether she could rip them off, as he had done to hers, but then decided that if it didn't work it would ruin everything that had built up between them.

Instead, she began a line of kisses from his chest to his navel, following the pattern he had set, feeling a smile of triumph when he groaned and squirmed. 'What are you doing to me?' he asked gruffly.

Rhianne didn't answer. His hands were on her head, threading once again through the thickness of her hair so that he could hold her hard against him. Inching his briefs down, she nibbled each area of skin as it was exposed. The roughness of his hair tickled her nose, and when she found her goal Rhianne almost began to wish that she hadn't started this. It was a totally new experience, and it was instinct alone that drove her.

Zarek felt as though he'd died and gone to heaven, but he also knew the danger of allowing the situation to get out of hand. He'd urged Rhianne into it, and if she was enjoying herself too much then it was his fault. But he didn't want her throwing everything back in his face afterwards.

He used a few choice Greek phrases. There was only so much a man could stand, and he was reaching the end of his limit. 'Rhianne, please stop.'

She turned her eyes up towards his face. 'You do not like what I am doing?' She looked hurt and vulnerable, and he crushed her head against him. But he hadn't stopped to think, and her lips encountered again the part of him that throbbed like hell and was ready to leap out of control.

Immediately he let her go, and when she looked at him this time her eyes were so luminous he thought they must be awash with tears. Hell, why had he stopped her? She so clearly wasn't averse to kissing him in this manner, and he hated the thought that she'd done it to some other man. But she must have done because otherwise how would she have known what to do? She had touched and kissed him in exactly the right spots to send his testosterone levels shooting sky high.

This wasn't the way he had intended the evening to go. He had wanted to take it slowly, much more slowly, probably lasting the whole night through. Instead,

Rhianne was drawing him so close to the edge that it could all be over in a matter of minutes.

'It's not that I don't like it, *agapi mou*, but I wanted us to take things more slowly; I wanted to—oh, God, what am I saying? I want you now, desperately.' Without another word he lifted her up and dropped her on the bed, sweeping chocolates aside with one swift movement of his hand.

His breathing was deep and out of control as he kicked off his briefs that Rhianne had so tantalizingly entered. Free of all restrictions, he lowered himself on the bed beside her. Her shoes had fallen off but she still wore the sheer stockings with the delicate lacy tops, and just the sight of them on her amazingly long legs was like receiving a kick in the gut.

He found it hard to breathe now, and for the moment he wanted to feast his eyes on her. She looked incredibly beautiful: her eyes dreamy, her fantastic auburn hair fanned out over the pillow, her lips parted expectantly, just the tip of her tongue showing as she moistened them.

His own mouth was dry; he knew exactly how she felt. This was a significant moment for both of them. He trailed a finger from the pulse at the base of her throat, encircling her breasts, watching as her nipples seemed to spring into even more vibrant life, but he didn't touch them, much as he wanted to, much as he knew Rhianne wanted him to do. No, his fingers were on a different journey. They traced a path over her belly button, pausing a moment to explore its creases, then moved ever lower, entwining now in the softness of her hair which excited him by being the same shade as the hair on her head.

When he reached his goal, Rhianne bucked and tight-ened beneath his touch. She was so ready for him that all his thoughts about exciting her some more flew out of the window. Time for that another day. Nothing was needed now except the uniting of their bodies. Waiting would be agony for both of them.

But he had one last question. 'You are all right with this?' he asked as he turned his back on her for a moment to pull on a condom.

Rhianne gave the faintest of nods. Her throat was so tight that she couldn't have spoken had she wanted to. She was more than ready. Her whole body ached to be possessed. Nothing else existed in the whole world except the two of them, here, now, in this beautiful room. She didn't know what Zarek had done to her, but she wanted him with something approaching desperation. If this was what making love was all about then why had she waited so long?

Zarek entered her carefully and slowly, even though she knew he probably wanted to take her fiercely and sensationally. She appreciated his thoughtfulness but she too was hungry, and she raised her hips in instinctive invitation.

With a deep-throated groan he slid his hands beneath her bottom and urged her even closer. He hesitated only briefly when his entry was restricted, too far gone then to stop, and besides Rhianne didn't want him to. The pain was gone in an instant, and it seemed like only seconds before her whole world exploded, sensations such as she had never felt before chasing through every inch of her in wave after wave. Moments later Zarek reached his own climax. His body jerked and throbbed on top of her, and it was a lifetime before he found the strength to roll away.

Rhianne had never felt like this in her whole life. Euphoric was a word that came to mind. Stunned, as well, that such magic could take place. And in that

moment came the realisation that she had fallen deeply
and irrevocably in love with Zarek.

But her euphoria didn't last long. Not allowing himself
the pleasure of glorying in the feelings that must have filled
him too, Zarek jumped off the bed and glared down at her.

'Why the hell didn't you tell me that you were a virgin?'

CHAPTER TWELVE

RHIANNE'S eyes dimmed with tears. What did it matter that this had been the first time for her? Hadn't he enjoyed it? Wasn't she good enough? Had he expected more? She turned her face away from him, feeling as though her heart was about to break. For the very first time in her life she had given herself to a man, freely and joyfully, and now he was throwing accusations at her.

'I didn't think it was important.'

'Not important?' he asked angrily. 'The first time is special for every woman.'

'And you think that wasn't special for me?' she asked sharply, her head jerking back so that her eyes could glare into his. She wished that she knew what he was saying. He was ruining what had been the most beautiful experience of her life.

'I'd like to think it was, but…' He shook his head again as though trying to rid it of unholy thoughts. 'You should have told me. I thought that you and—'

'No!' Rhianne cut in swiftly, adding without thinking, 'I always swore I'd remain a virgin until I married.'

Zarek dropped his head into his hands. 'What have I done?'

'It's not your fault,' insisted Rhianne swiftly. 'I wanted it as much as you.'

'But—'

'But nothing,' she cut in fiercely. She wasn't going to let him ruin this exquisite moment. 'I wanted it too, Zarek. I was ready.'

'I don't understand.' His dark eyes bored into hers, trying to read the reasoning behind her change of mind.

'I don't understand either,' she answered. 'All I know is that I've never felt like this in my whole life. I've discovered that I didn't know what I was missing.'

Zarek snorted, and after one further glare in her direction he marched across the room.

Rhianne felt like crying. Her fantastic experience was turning into a nightmare. She had wanted this night to go on and on. She had even forgotten for a while that their marriage was only make-believe, something Zarek had dreamt up to save the future of his company.

If that was the case then he shouldn't have encouraged her. He should have left her alone. She hadn't asked for any of it.

Anger began to pulse through her veins now, and she went after him. 'Don't think you can walk away and make me feel the guilty party,' she yelled.

He turned and looked at her with eyes so bleak that they scared her. 'You should have told me,' was all he said before leaving the room and closing the door resolutely in her face.

Zarek felt sick to the very core of him. He had done the unforgivable. He knew that some women didn't think twice about losing their virginity, but Rhianne was different. Rhianne had been saving herself for the one man she fell deeply in love with and ultimately married, and he applauded her for that.

Now he had ruined everything.

Whichever way he looked at it their marriage wasn't real. He had forced her into it. He'd like to think that he had persuaded her but, no, he had taken advantage when her defences were low.

He would never forgive himself.

Downstairs he poured himself another glass of champagne before setting the bottle down on the table so loudly that he didn't hear the door open or Rhianne step inside. The first he knew of her presence was when her hand touched his shoulder.

'If you're feeling as bad as I am then I'm glad,' she said briskly, her blue eyes filled with fighting spirit.

He turned to look at her, and his heart lurched agonisingly. Oh, Lord, he wanted to take her again, and knowing that it was now forbidden was like someone hammering a nail into his head.

'But the fact remains that I knew exactly what I was doing when I allowed you to—' her voice faltered for a second '—make love to me. And I don't regret it. If you do, that's your prerogative, but your anger is badly misplaced.'

Zarek turned away from her, moving to look out the window. The courtyard was in darkness, and it suited his mood. A few stars winked in the sky, but he could see nothing else except Rhianne's reflection in the glass. He tapped his fingertips together. She looked so hauntingly sad. He wanted to apologise profusely, but at the same time he wanted her in his arms and in his bed again.

Desire fought with honour.

Conscience fought with craving.

He watched in fascination as she moved slowly towards him, each footstep silent and wary, totally oblivious to the fact that he could see her in the glass. His heart hammered at an alarming rate, so loud that it echoed in his ears, so loud that he felt sure Rhianne must hear it too.

It seemed to fill the room, and he knew that he was in danger of forgetting his good intentions. Once he touched her again he would not be able to let her go, and they would end up sharing his bed for the rest of the night.

When she was almost upon him, when he couldn't bear to watch her any longer, he spun around. Immediately she grew as still as a statue—nothing moved except her eyes. They had turned almost navy, and deep down inside them he saw his own pain mirrored, his own need mirrored. She didn't speak, she didn't do anything except look at him.

'You know what I want from you?' he asked, his voice harsher than he'd intended.

Rhianne nodded, the movement so slight that he almost missed it.

'You also know I'm not offering you anything permanent? Once the business is safe you'll be free to go your own way. To find yourself a man to love. To settle down and have children.' Why did these words hurt when Rhianne meant nothing to him?

Except that she did. She meant more to him than he dared admit. But she was doing him a favour, that was all. She would be well rewarded.

She had also been a virgin, prompted his conscience.

Zarek cringed. He needed no reminding of what he had done. But what was done couldn't be undone, and if Rhianne was willing to share his bed for the duration of their marriage then he would be a fool to deny himself the pleasure.

'I knew what I was taking on when I agreed to marry you,' said Rhianne quietly.

'You didn't know that I expected you to be my lover.'

'Well, no,' she agreed, 'but having done so once it would be cruel of me to deny you the pleasure again.'

'Even though I've taken what has to be a woman's most important virtue?'

Rhianne nodded. 'I guess the right man never came along.'

Zarek frowned, alarm bells ringing. 'And you're saying that I'm the right man?'

'You touched the right button, Zarek, that is all.' Rhianne knew that she dared not let him see how she truly felt. Not when it was the last thing in the world that he wanted. He was a normal, healthy male who needed a woman in his bed. Not a woman to love, to keep by his side for the rest of his life, but someone to feed his natural hunger.

'You set me alive,' she said now. 'No other man's ever done that. You've shown me how much pleasure there is in making love. I don't regret saving myself all these years, but neither do I regret letting you take my virginity.'

Throwing caution to the wind, Rhianne flung herself at him. 'I want to make love again, Zarek, and again and again.' She lifted her mouth up to his, and with a groan he gathered her to him.

The rest of the night passed in a blur of lovemaking and sleeping, one became entwined with the other, and when Rhianne finally opened her eyes to bright blue skies and an empty bed beside her all she did was smile satisfyingly and curl up again.

But not for long. Wide awake now, she flung back the covers and walked out to the terrace, stretching her arms up high and appreciating the warmth of the sun on her naked body. It felt good to be alive.

She didn't hear Zarek return; she knew nothing until she felt his arms around her slender waist, holding her against his hard body which was again burning with need. His hands moved to cup her breasts, and she sank her head back on his shoulder.

'How are you this morning, Rhianne *mou*?'

His voice was thickly accented, the Greek in him coming to the fore. It was also incredibly sexy, and she twisted in his arms and raised her lips up to his. 'I feel wonderful,' she said. 'I'd go so far as to say that I've never felt like this in my whole life.'

Zarek groaned and kissed her hard and long. 'Breakfast is ready if you're hungry.'

'I'm hungry for you,' she murmured, gyrating her hips against him, exulting when she felt his immediate arousal. Heaven help her, but she wanted him again, now, urgently. As if she hadn't had enough of him during the night! It was as though once she'd discovered the potential in lovemaking she couldn't get enough of it.

'*Agapi mou*,' he said softly, 'there isn't time for this. Breakfast awaits us in the courtyard and you need to shower. I'll see you there.' He disentangled himself from her embrace, and Rhianne pulled a sad face.

'We could shower together.'

'Don't tempt me,' he groaned. 'I've already showered and I need to phone the hospital.'

'I thought your father looked remarkably well yesterday,' said Rhianne. So well, in fact, that she feared he would surprise them all and live for ever. And the longer their marriage lasted the harder it was going to be to walk away when he had no further use for her. Just one night spent in Zarek's bed had taught her that she never wanted to let him go.

'That is the trouble; he can look a picture of health when indeed he is suffering. And you'll be wanting to see your mother again this morning, of course.'

In consideration that it had been their first night as man and wife, her mother had stayed at Zarek's family home. His mother, of course, had been pleased to have company because Christos and his wife had declined her invitation, declaring that they needed to get back home.

'How long is she staying?'

Rhianne had no idea. 'I don't think she's in any particular rush. But won't your parents expect us to go away on honeymoon?' she asked hesitantly, her stomach churning at the very thought of them going off somewhere on their own. Not that they weren't alone here, but there was always his family to be considered.

'Not with my father so ill. I've told my mother that we're putting it on hold; she understands. Are you disappointed, Rhianne?'

His voice was deep and gruff, and he looked so deeply into her eyes, as if trying to see right into her mind, that Rhianne shook her head quickly. 'Of course not. Like you said last night, ours isn't a proper marriage. A honeymoon would be farcical.'

'Precisely,' he said, his voice taking on an odd inflection as he swung quickly away and left the room.

He wanted her body but he didn't want her, thought Rhianne as she hurried along to her own room to shower and dress. It was a disturbing thought, but there was nothing she could do except make the most of the situation. Zarek was unashamedly using her—and she was unashamedly letting him! That was all there was to it.

Breakfast consisted of coffee and *koulouraki*—delicious biscuits, some studded with nuts and raisins, others flavored with cinnamon, cloves and nutmeg. Zarek didn't seem hungry, and neither was she if the truth were known, delicious though the biscuits were.

He seemed to be brooding over something. 'Is your father worse?' she asked softly, that being the only reason she could think of for his mood. 'Was yesterday too much for him?'

He looked at her as if she were a stranger before shaking his head. 'I'm sorry. What did you say?'

'I was asking about your father.'

'Oh, yes. He's very tired this morning, but according to the nurse he's in good spirits.'

Because he knew that the company was now going to fall into the right hands, thought Rhianne. His father had told her time and time again yesterday how happy he was that Zarek was finally getting married, unaware that it was a plot they'd conceived to save the business. If he ever found out that his son felt no love for her, and that their marriage would be dissolved as soon as he died, it would be enough to kill him off far earlier than anyone anticipated.

'So what's on your mind?' she asked. 'Are you still beating yourself up for taking my—'

'No!' He said it with such vehemence that Rhianne knew he was lying. But she also knew that it would be fatal to question him further. If Zarek had demons he had to deal with them himself.

From her own personal point of view she wasn't at all sorry for what they had done. Zarek had taught her so much about her body and the way it could react that she wanted to skip and sing and tell the whole world about it.

'I'd like to go and see my mother,' she said. 'Find out what her plans are.'

'Naturally. I will drop you off there on my way to the hospital.'

In the end there was no need. They had just finished breakfast when a taxi arrived. Her mother looked radiant. 'I've just had a phone call from David. He's apologised profusely for letting me down. He's promised it won't happen again. He says it was the biggest mistake of his life. I'm flying home today; I hope you don't mind.'

Rhianne hugged her tightly. Her mother's happiness meant a lot to her. 'Not at all. I've always thought he was the right man for you.'

After her mother left, saying she already had a flight booked, Rhianne went in search of Zarek, only to discover that he had already left for the hospital.

She sat down, feeling deflated. He could have told her. Why hadn't he? Why had he slipped away so silently? His mood this morning was an enigma. Whereas she had been full of the joys of life, he had retreated into himself.

Now she was bored. There was nothing for her to do. She was stuck here without a car or companionship. Even his housekeeper had disappeared. She resented this place now. It was undeniably beautiful, but it was not some-where to be alone. Especially the day after her wedding!

On an impulse she decided to jump into Zarek's Jacuzzi. Would their night of passion be a one-off, she asked herself as she switched on the tub and climbed into the pulsing water. Or would he want her to share his bed every night from now on?

Her eyes were closed when she heard the sound, and when she snapped them open it was to see Zarek standing in front of her, stark naked, his clothes on the floor at his feet.

'Were you waiting for me?' he asked, stepping into the hot tub as casually as if he was sharing a car with her.

'I had nothing else to do,' she claimed, determined not to give him the privilege of seeing how her heart leapt at the sight of him, how it thudded in her breast as though it wanted to escape and hook up with his.

'Where is your mother?'

'She left shortly after you.'

'In that case, I'm sorry for leaving you. I thought she would want to spend time with you.'

'She's going back to David. They're making up. I hope it lasts this time. Your parents are a good example of true love; I admire them. I would like to think that—' Rhianne stopped, suddenly realising what she'd been going to say.

Zarek nodded slowly. 'Let us hope that one day you too will meet the right man.'

But I already have, don't you know that? she questioned silently. She wanted no one else. She was truly convinced that no one in the whole world could make her feel the way that Zarek did. She was consumed by an unbelievable passion whenever he was near.

Like now!

She wanted to inch closer to him, she wanted his arms around her; she wanted his kisses; more than anything, she wanted to taste his mouth, his skin. Even thinking about it drew a response deep down in her stomach, and she was glad he could not see her wriggling on the narrow seat. The force of the jets hid the tremors that ran through her, but as well as hiding they intensified her feelings.

Zarek, on the other hand, sat there looking as cool as if they were sitting in church. He gave nothing away. He'd got her now, thought Rhianne miserably. He'd married and bedded her and had her where he wanted her. He didn't have to try any more; he knew that she would remain loyal until such time as the business fell into his hands.

Quite how it happened Rhianne didn't know, but when Zarek's thigh unexpectedly touched hers she pulled back sharply. She dared not let him touch her because there was no way she could hold back on the hunger that filled every pulsing inch of her.

Zarek knew that his fears were confirmed. Rhianne had done her duty by him, but now that she'd had time to think about it she didn't want him to even touch her any more. It was hard to believe this after last night. Had it all been an act? Had she forced herself to respond to him?

No, it had been real, he was sure of that. But in the time they'd been apart she'd come to her senses and realised that giving herself to him so wildly and innocently could have far-reaching consequences.

He could understand her feelings because hadn't he been cross with himself this morning? Yet she had been the one who had come begging for more, and he'd have had to be a very strong man indeed to turn her away. Their lovemaking had been wild and exciting, in fact he would dare go so far as to say that he'd never met a woman who reacted so wonderfully, who seemed to know instinctively what he wanted her to do. For a virgin she'd been dynamite.

But he most certainly couldn't sit here and not touch her. 'It's time I took you on another tour of the island,' he said decisively, getting to his feet. 'You've seen very little of it so far.'

Rhianne gulped at the sight of his nakedness so near to her face. Her awareness trebled in microseconds, shooting tremors through every cell and causing her whole body to set on fire. She didn't want a tour, she wanted to stay here and make love.

But Zarek's face was stern; she really had no option.

She waited until he had moved through to his bedroom before she stepped out of the tub, then realised that she didn't have a towel or a robe. All she could do was pretend that it did not bother her. She stood tall and proud, her chin high, her eyes straight ahead as she walked past him. It was not until she reached the door that he called her name. Rhianne halted but did not turn.

'Rhianne,' he said again softly.

She turned her head.

'Where are you going?'

'To get dressed.'

'You look stunning as you are.'

'If we're to go out, then—' She got no further.

With a deep guttural growl Zarek closed the space between them. 'You tempt me too hard. I told myself I wouldn't take advantage of you again. But then you parade in front of me as naked as the day you were born. What is a man supposed to do?'

'Close his eyes,' said Rhianne, feeling her breath begin to come in short bursts. Zarek had pulled on a pair of boxers and therefore had the advantage. Heat spread through her with amazing speed, starting at the very core of her before reaching its long tentacles to reach every cell in her body.

'Impossible,' he declared. 'And since you're my wife I think I have every right to feast my eyes on you. Turn around, Rhianne.'

Slowly she did as he asked, trying to ignore the butter-flies in her stomach, trying to keep still as he took in the way her nipples stood proud and erect—and ready. The way little goose bumps rose all over her skin despite the heat. The way she kept her chin high and her eyes on his.

Not by the merest flinch was she going to let him see that she was seriously aroused. There were some things she could do nothing about, but what was happening inside her—blood racing madly through her veins, pulses working overtime, her mouth drying up—these things she could hide.

But not for long!

Enough was enough. The way his sensational golden-brown eyes appraised every inch of her body sent her senses spinning into space, and with her eyes now locked into his, she sashayed her way towards him. She couldn't help herself; everything seemed to be happening of its own accord.

Zarek's groan was deeper than she'd ever heard it. Their ride out was forgotten. They tumbled onto the bed, and where Zarek's eyes had roved, kisses now peppered her skin. Kissing and sucking, nipping and grazing. Her whole world felt as though it had fallen off its orbit. Where his mouth touched, her skin burned, her head rocking from side to side in an attempt to deny herself such pleasure. It was impossible.

'Zarek…'

'Rhianne?' For a fraction of a second his eyes met hers, seeing her torment, delighting in it. He covered her mouth with his, his tongue urgent, seeking, touching, tormenting, creating a fresh stream of emotions that were almost too much to bear. Then it was off again on another exploration. There was not one inch of her body that he did not investigate, did not taste, did not set on fire, but when Rhianne attempted to turn the tables, when she wanted to touch and explore and kiss him he was having none of it.

Instead, he spread her legs and lowered himself over her, his eyes never leaving hers. The only sound that could be heard was their heavy breathing—and the telephone!

Rhianne wanted him to ignore it. She was fast approaching the point of no return. He couldn't leave her like this.

Zarek swore loudly, but he nevertheless reached out for his phone where it sat on the bedside table. In seconds he was on his feet.

'I'm needed at the hospital,' he said bluntly.

CHAPTER THIRTEEN

ZAREK'S heart and mind were in turmoil as he drove to the hospital. Rhianne had begged to come with him, but she'd already driven him half crazy; he needed time alone to clear his head.

And the news wasn't good when he got there. His mother was in tears, and his father was critical. He telephoned Rhianne to tell her that he was staying for as long as his mother needed him—and then during the night his father passed away.

Although they had known it was coming, his mother was inconsolable. Zarek took her home and sent a car to fetch Rhianne. His brother arrived as well, and Zarek was annoyed that he hadn't even made it to the hospital. He kept the peace, though, for his mother's sake, and in the days that followed there was nothing but sadness in the Diakos villa.

Rhianne helped wherever she could and was invited to stay in the room when the lawyer came to the house to read the will. As Zarek had told her, the business would now fall into his hands.

'So what do I get out of it?' asked a very cross Christos. 'This is ridiculous; it should be shared between us.'

'Have you ever had anything to do with it?' asked Zarek coldly.

'Well, no, but—'

'Your father's left you a considerable sum of money,' said the lawyer.

'And you'll get this house when I die,' explained his mother.

But Christos still felt that the biggest share of his father's estate was going to Zarek, and he didn't bother to hide his jealous anger.

A few days later, when his mother announced that she was going to stay with her sister for a while, Rhianne and Zarek returned to the villa.

By this time Rhianne was absolutely convinced that she had now served her purpose. Not once during the time they'd spent at his parents' house had Zarek made love to her. He'd not even kissed her. He'd lain by her side in bed, and although she knew that sometimes he wasn't asleep, he hadn't spoken, or touched her even.

He was upset that his father was gone, and she would have liked to comfort him, but unless he turned to her she did not feel it was something she could do. He was locked in his own world of grief in which she had no part to play. If it had been a real marriage he might have turned to her for comfort, but as things were…

Sadness enveloped her. She had made the mistake of falling in love with Zarek. She hadn't realised quite how deeply until this moment, and it broke her heart to think that any day soon he would tell her that she was no longer needed.

'What are your plans now?' she asked, as they sat outside after dinner. The air was heavy with the scent of honeysuckle, a dog barked and another answered, there was the usual distant bray of a donkey, but there was total silence between them.

'I'm going back to England,' he announced. 'For a while, at least. There's no point in me staying here while my mother's away.'

And how about me, she wanted to ask. Will I be returning to your apartment with you, or will you give me a lump sum of money and tell me that I'm on my own now? It was what he had promised her. He had no other obligations. As far as he was concerned she had done what he'd asked. Otherwise why was he leaving her severely alone?

A tear trickled down her cheek, and Rhianne jumped up, intending to go to her room, surprised when Zarek reached out and grabbed her arm. 'Stay with me. I want— Rhianne, you're crying! What is wrong?'

'A weak moment,' she answered, with a wry twist to her lips. 'It's been a sad few days.'

Zarek nodded. 'My father was my best friend; I shall miss him.'

'Of course you will,' she said softly. 'At least you made him a happy man towards the end.'

'But I married you for mercenary reasons. I wasn't being fair on you, Rhianne. Naturally, I will—'

'Pay me for my services?' She lifted her chin and smiled. No way was she going to let him see how upset she was. 'Thank me for a job well done? It was my pleasure, Zarek, but I'm looking forward now to a new life of my own. I might even move away from London. Make a start somewhere else.'

Zarek's grip on her arm tightened, and he drew her

towards him. 'You don't have to do this, Rhianne. We can work something out. I don't want you to—'

'It's not a matter of what you want any longer, Zarek, it's what I want.' She kept her voice terse and allowed herself to look straight into his eyes, then wished she hadn't when she felt the familiar lurching of her senses.

But she was no longer his, not in the true sense of the word, and she wished now that she had never let him make love to her because the end of their marriage could have come so much more quickly with an annulment.

'And what do you want, Rhianne?' he asked quietly.

'Didn't you hear me, Zarek? I want a life of my own.'

A shield came down in front of his eyes. They were impassive now, and there was no expression in his voice when he spoke. 'So be it. I shall be sorry to let you go, but…'

Sorry to let her go! Because she was good in bed? Because she was an excellent secretary? But not because he loved her! Which was what she wanted most.

He enjoyed making love to her, but he was not in love with her. It was a bittersweet thought. With Zarek at her side for the rest of her life she could have climbed mountains. He was a strong, capable man, caring as well as mercenary, and he would have always been there for her.

Now she had a future to face on her own because it was doubtful she would ever find anyone else to fill his shoes. He had taken her heart and made it his own, and when she walked away from him she would be leaving it behind.

She suddenly realised that he had let go of her arm. She was simply standing there, looking at him, imprinting every tiny detail of his face into her memory so that she could take it out occasionally and think about what might have been.

'But what?' she enquired, suddenly remembering that he had tailed off mid-sentence.

'The ultimate decision is yours; that's what I was going to say. It's a woman's prerogative to change her mind.'

'I shan't,' she declared firmly.

'Then we'll fly home tomorrow. You'll stay with me, of course, until you find a place of your own, which I shall buy for you, naturally. I'll also see to it that there are sufficient funds in your bank account to—'

'*Stop!*' Rhianne held up hand. 'I don't want all of this, just enough to tide me over until I find another job and somewhere to rent.'

'A promise is a promise, Rhianne.'

'And promises are made to be broken.'

'Not by me. You gave up your life for me, Rhianne. You'll never know how much I appreciate it. And although it was for a shorter time than I expected, I shall honour my word. And that is final.'

So let him, she thought, Let him waste his money on her. It would actually be a small price to pay when she had given him something that she had prized for so long.

She would never feel the same again as far as making love was concerned. No other man would ever make her fly with the stars or ride on the moon. She had discovered secrets about herself that she could have never guessed. Precious secrets. Precious memories.

'If that is your wish, Zarek. I'm going to bed now. Goodnight.'

'Goodnight, Rhianne. Sleep well.'

Zarek found it hard to believe that Rhianne wanted to leave him so soon. He had thought, mistakenly it would appear, that Rhianne had begun to feel something for him. Would she have given herself to him so willingly otherwise?

How could he have got it so wrong?

He had even begun to think that she was falling in love with him. How stupid was that? All she'd felt was the excitement of making love. He had taught her how to appreciate her body, and she had used it to full advantage.

He had always known that their deal would end one day; what he hadn't counted on was that he would actually fall in love with Rhianne in the process. He didn't want to let her go—*ever*. But he was faced with the fact that Rhianne didn't return his love.

It was with an aching heart that he let her go. What he really wanted to do was follow her up to her room and throw caution to the winds. He wanted to make love to her so fiercely that it would drown out all his unhappy thoughts. He wanted to lose himself in her body and—

Zarek suddenly realised that he was thinking of himself again. His needs, his unhappiness. He wasn't thinking about Rhianne. She had every right to want to walk free. It was part of their contract. And if he didn't do the right thing and let her go, he would have to live with it for the rest of his life.

Rhianne had made it very clear that she didn't love him. She had discovered the thrill of lovemaking, but it would now be the turn of some other man to win her heart and enjoy everything that he had taught her.

Anger filled Zarek now. Had taking over the family business really been worth forcing Rhianne to marry him? What had he been thinking? How brainless was he? His fingers curled and uncurled, and every breath he took filled him with even more fury.

In the end he tore off his clothes and dived into the pool, swimming length after length after length until he could physically do no more. He collapsed onto one of the canvas loungers and remained there until the first fingers of dawn appeared in the sky, when he forced himself up to his room to shower and dress.

By this time his mind had cleared. He knew exactly what he had to do.

During the flight home Rhianne buried her head in a book, though she didn't read a single word. The letters danced before her eyes like gnats on a hot summer night. Zarek had rescued her out of a desperate situation, but now she was on her own. She had to find somewhere to live and a job to pay for it. Although Zarek had insisted that he would provide her with a home, she was not counting on it.

This morning he had barely spoken. His lips were tight and grim, and he looked as though he hadn't been to sleep. Which could be because of his father, or it might be because he was now faced with the problem of house-hunting on her behalf. Not that he would do it personally; any one of his minions could take on the job. It was something he might ask his secretary to do—except that she was his temporary secretary. In all the excitement she had forgotten. Would he expect her to continue working for him? And if so how difficult would that be?

Endless thoughts chased through her mind, and she was glad when the plane touched down. They were met by his chauffeur and taken straight to Zarek's penthouse.

There was no escape here either. The big blue skies of Greece were replaced by leaden grey ones. And although the apartment was sumptuous, with plenty of space and its own terrace garden, it felt like a prison. There was no aquamarine sea to look out over. No outdoor pool to laze away the days by. Whereas once she had felt intoxicated by it all, now she was anxious to get away.

'I'm going to the office,' Zarek told her, still with no smile on his face. Nothing but a frown tugging his brows together and no expression at all in his handsome dark eyes.

'Do you need me?' she asked quickly.

His brows rose questioningly. 'If you feel up to it, you can start work again tomorrow,' he answered, with a quick shake of his head. 'For now I want you to relax. The last few days can't have been easy for you either.'

You'll never know how hard they've been, Rhianne thought. Hiding the love she felt for this man was the hardest thing she'd ever had to do.

But once he'd gone, and the apartment was empty, Rhianne began to wish that she'd insisted on joining him. There was nothing to do. She could go window shopping. Or a walk in Hyde Park. But neither of these options appealed.

She sat down with the same book that she'd tried to read on the plane, but ten minutes later she still hadn't turned a page. She watched a butterfly dancing in the breeze. She heard the drone of a plane high overhead. Then her cell phone rang.

Her first thought was that it was Zarek—until she realised that he would use the house phone if he needed to speak to her. Then she recognised Annie's number. The first time her so-called friend had called since the day Rhianne had found her in the arms of her fiancé. For a few seconds she was tempted not to answer. Annie was the cause of everything that had happened to her. But there were things that needed to be said.

'Rhianne,' said Annie at once. 'Where have you been? I've been trying to get in touch with you for ages.'

'So that you can apologise? Tell me that it was a mistake? That you'll never do it again? Forgive me, Annie, for not wanting to listen. I thought you were my best friend. I thought—'

'Rhianne,' interrupted Annie. 'I admit I made the biggest mistake of my life. But it wasn't all my fault. Angus practically forced himself on me. And I've always fancied him, as you know. He told me that you two had fallen out and—'

'He was lying,' cut in Rhianne fiercely. 'I don't really wish to continue this conversation, Annie. I have a new life now—and you're not a part of it.'

Her thumb hovered, preparing to cut the call short, and as though Annie knew what was happening she cried, 'No, wait! You have to accept my apology. I didn't set out to hurt you. I had to go away, and when I got back you'd disappeared off the face of the earth. Your phone was never switched on and no one knew where you were.'

'Actually,' said Rhianne, 'I was getting married, to the most amazing man. So if you see Angus again you can tell him that.' And this time she did end the call. She also switched off her phone.

Zarek arrived home in the middle of the afternoon. Rhianne wasn't expecting him until much later, and her heart went into spasm at the sight of him. In his dark, exquisitely tailored suit and white shirt he looked very much the businessman again—a complete contrast to the casually dressed man who had won her heart in Santorini.

Whatever he wore, though, whether it was swimming trunks or his wedding suit, he was just as incredibly sexy. It oozed from his pores, and simply looking at him made her want to share his bed again.

'Has everything run smoothly in your absence?' she enquired, hoping her voice didn't give away her inner turmoil.

'Actually, yes,' he answered. 'Which proves I have good staff running my office. I've also heard that my secretary has decided not to return to work. Motherhood suits her, apparently.'

'So you'll be looking for someone else?' Rhianne wondered why the thought of no longer working for Zarek felt like a knot tightening in her belly. She had known the day would come when their paths took them different ways; indeed, she had intended it so, but she had thought there might be a winding down process.

'As a matter of fact,' he said, his eyes watchful on her face, causing further *frissons* of awareness to rush through her veins as though they were in a race all by themselves, 'I'm offering you the job. I know you were talking about moving away, but you'll never find another position as well paid. You've told me that you enjoy the work; therefore, it makes sound economical sense.'

His eyes were more gold than brown as they locked into hers, and Rhianne felt a further tortuous spiral of awareness, which she swiftly slammed back down.

'And as promised I'll find you somewhere to live—though it has to be a decent house—not a poky little apartment like the one you used to live in. In the meantime your home is here.'

Rhianne swallowed hard. 'You're more than generous,

Zarek, but it really isn't necessary.' How could she go on working and living with him while loving him at the same time? It might make economical sense, but not common sense. Not where her heart was concerned. Or her sanity. Or her feelings. It would be fatal.

'I think it is,' he said. 'There is no way that I can throw you out now and leave you to fend for yourself.'

'You make me sound like a cat,' she said, trying to make a joke of it, but aware that she failed miserably.

'I happen to love cats,' he answered, a quick, whimsical smile playing about his lips. 'But the fact remains, Rhianne, that I can never repay you enough for what you've done. The least I can do is ensure that you're both comfortable and financially sound. But it all takes time.'

'You could pay me off and I'll find my own job and somewhere to live,' she ventured, though it wasn't really what she wanted to do. But staying here with him, loving him, knowing it wasn't reciprocated, was going to be the hardest thing she had ever done.

'Rhianne, I feel totally responsible for you, and until…' his voice tailed off, a closed look crossing his face '…until such time as you have somewhere else to live, until I've seen to it that you have no money worries—or any other worries for that matter—then I insist you remain here.'

Rhianne felt sure that he had been going to say something else, but she knew better than to ask. She lifted her shoulders instead. 'You're the boss.'

Zarek wanted to be more than her boss. He wanted to be her lover, her husband and her best friend all rolled into one. He wanted to be the father of her children. He wanted to spend the rest of his life with her.

He had never felt like this about any other woman. He'd gone to work today not for the reason he'd told Rhianne, but because he'd needed to get away so that he could think. When she'd said that she wanted to move out and begin again without him, he had felt distraught.

If he didn't want to spend the rest of his life regretting letting her slip away, he had to do something about it *now*. He fought battles all the time in the boardroom. This was no different. His plan had been to take things slowly, but he was not sure there was time. Give Rhianne an excuse and she would be off.

'I thought we'd eat out this evening,' he said to her now. 'I've booked a table at—'

'If I'm working tomorrow I'd like an early night,' she said quickly, her chin jutting in that determined way he was beginning to recognise.

'We don't have to be late, Rhianne.'

'I'd still prefer to stay in,' she declared, her blue eyes challenging his now.

If they did, he wouldn't be responsible for what happened. It was safe to go out, but eating here, having a few drinks, sitting so close to her that he could smell the tempting fragrance of her body, he wasn't sure that he could handle it.

She was far too dangerous.

'You drive a hard bargain, Rhianne.'

'I don't see why you should continue to spend money on me when my job is over.'

Zarek was aghast. She was clearly determined that they had reached the end of their agreement. From now on it was pure business as far as she was concerned.

'Maybe our business deal has come to an end,' he

agreed, 'but it doesn't mean to say that we can't still be—friends.' It was not a word he wanted to use. She was his lover and his wife, and he was determined that she would stay that way. 'Tell me, Rhianne, the true reason you seem anxious to see as little of me as possible. Why you want to walk away so quickly.'

He waited a long time for her answer. In fact he thought she wasn't going to answer at all. First of all she avoided looking at him, staring out the window instead. Then she drew in a deep breath and faced him, her eyes filled with such sorrow that he couldn't help himself.

In less than a second he closed the space between them, took her into his arms and held her tightly against his chest. 'Rhianne, what is wrong?'

Her whole body trembled, and he was fearful that she was perhaps ill and hadn't told him about it. He stroked her hair, he felt the racing pulse in her temple, and he crushed her against him even harder.

Suddenly she tilted her head to look up at him, and when he saw the vulnerability in her eyes he couldn't stop himself. He lowered his head and kissed her, a long, hard kiss from which she had no escape. He didn't want her to escape. He wanted to show her how much he cared.

Rhianne returned his kiss with a passion that excited him, but when he pulled away so that he could look into her face and wonder what was happening, he saw tears. He asked her again, 'What is wrong, Rhianne?'

Rhianne knew that she had no choice but to tell Zarek the truth. If she didn't, she would go on wondering for the rest of her life whether she had made a huge mistake. It was a case of humiliation now because he didn't return her love. Or the chance of a lifetime's happiness.

She had sensed a change in Zarek since he'd returned from the office. Prior to that she'd felt there was no point in hanging around. But now he was making it clear that he didn't want her to go. Dared she hope that he'd fallen in love with her too?

Closing her eyes, not wanting to see his reaction, she said faintly, 'I'm sorry, Zarek, but I've fallen in love with you. I know you didn't want it but—'

He gave her no chance to say any more. With a deep groan Zarek's mouth crushed hers yet again in a kiss that ended with them both gasping for breath.

'Rhianne, *agapi mou*, you have no idea how happy you've just made me. I was dreading the thought of losing you.'

'You—you love me too?' she asked breathlessly, her eyes turning wide and almost navy in their surprise.

He nodded. 'With all of my heart.'

'You're not just saying that?'

'Rhianne,' he said softly, cupping her face with both hands and looking deep into her eyes. 'I've never said it to any other woman in my life. I guess I didn't believe in true love. I loved my work more. But you have given me something so rich and so beautiful that I never want to lose it. I adore you, my gorgeous wife. You're the best thing that's ever happened to me. I want to make babies with you, I want to live into my old age with you, I want to—'

'Stop!' Rhianne placed her finger over his lips. 'I need to ask you a question.'

Zarek smiled, a slow, warm smile that softened his entire face. 'Whatever you like, my darling.'

'Would you have let me go if I hadn't declared my love?' Rhianne held her breath as she waited for his answer. It was something she needed to know because if he said yes it would mean that he didn't love her as much as she loved him.

'It was my initial intention,' he admitted, with a wry twist to his lips. 'But then I realised that I couldn't do it. I could never let you go. I love you too deeply. I would have found some way of persuading you to fall in love with me—no matter how long it took.'

Rhianne gave a sigh of happy relief. 'Maybe I spoke too soon. I think I might have enjoyed the persuasion. Would it have gone something like this?' She draped her arms around his neck and pressed her soft lips against his in a kiss that took them both into a world where only happiness existed, a world where their future lay together—through thick and through thin—for ever more.

A beautiful collection of classic stories from
your favourite Mills & Boon® authors

With Love... Helen Bianchin
Bought Brides
This marriage was going
to happen...
Available 17th July 2009

With Love... Lynne Graham
Virgin Brides
A virgin for his pleasure!
Available 21st August 2009

With Love... Lucy Monroe
Royal Brides
Wed at his royal command!
Available 18th September 2009

With Love... Penny Jordan
Passionate Brides
Seduced...
Available 16th October 2009

Collect all four!

2 FREE,

BOOKS AND A SURPRISE GIFT!

We would like to take this opportunity to thank you for reading this Mills & Boon® book by offering you the chance to take TWO more specially selected titles from the Modern™ series absolutely FREE! We're also making this offer to introduce you to the benefits of the Mills & Boon® Book Club™—

- ★ **FREE home delivery**
- ★ **FREE gifts and competitions**
- ★ **FREE monthly Newsletter**
- ★ **Exclusive Mills & Boon Book Club offers**
- ★ **Books available before they're in the shops**

Accepting these FREE books and gift places you under no obligation to buy, you may cancel at any time, even after receiving your free shipment. Simply complete your details below and return the entire page to the address below. You don't even need a stamp!

YES! Please send me 2 free Modern books and a surprise gift. I understand that unless you hear from me, I will receive 4 superb new titles every month for just £3.19 each, postage and packing free. I am under no obligation to purchase any books and may cancel my subscription at any time. The free books and gift will be mine to keep in any case.

P9ZED

Ms/Mrs/Miss/Mr ....Initials ....

BLOCK CAPITALS PLEASE

Surname ....

Address ....

....

....Postcode................................

Send this whole page to:
UK: FREEPOST CN81, Croydon, CR9 3WZ